Love Can Heal

Gaylene Nunn

WEEZIE PUBLISHING

This book is dedicated to Donna Dobson, my best friend and sister by another set of parents. Her encouragement is never ending and her love for others knows no bounds.

Contents

Introduction

"Eventually, you will come to understand that love heals everything, and love is all there is." Gary Zukav

Ashley is bent over working on something between the cabin and the cistern when she hears someone walk up.

"Ashley, I want to talk about last night," Jeremy says harshly.

"Well, I don't. You had your chance last night," she replies in a strained voice.

"I've had time to calm down a little. I want to discuss why you said you couldn't kiss me."

Ashley takes a deep breath, stands upright, and turns to face Jeremy. She removes her gloves slowly, one at a time, glaring at Jeremy. Next, she removes her cap, placing the gloves inside the hat. "Fine. You want to talk? We'll talk," she yells. "Do you want to have this conversation out here or in the cabin?"

"I don't care," Jeremy yells back. "I want to know why you wouldn't kiss me when I asked you to?"

Even though Ashley glares at Jeremy in anger, her eyes fill with shame. "I wanted to kiss you, Jeremy. I wanted to so much, but I couldn't because I don't know how," Ashley whispers. "I'm twenty-six years old, and I've never kissed a man. You are the first man ever to kiss me. I'm sorry I disappointed you." Ashley throws her cap and gloves at Jeremy and walks off, hanging her head. She walks around the cabin and down into the valley, sits on a large boulder with her elbows on her knees, and sobs.

Chapter 1

ASHLEY

"Miss. Miss. You need to wake up." The voice sounds a million miles away. Ashley shifts her position but doesn't wake up. "Miss, you need to wake up now." The voice says, accompanied by a firm but gentle shake to her shoulder.

Ashley slowly opens her eyes and quickly realizes she is lying on a sofa with a man standing over her. "Oh, my gosh! What time is it?" she asks as the man backs away and Ashley sits up.

"Uh, it's 7:00. What are you doing here?" the man asks.

"Well, if it's any of your business, I was supposed to have an interview with Jarod Marsh at 4:00. It looks like he never showed up. I need to go." Ashley stands quickly and grabs her tote, declining to look at the man.

"Well, I assume Mr. Marsh was delayed. I'm sure you can call in the morning to reschedule," the man says.

"Nope. That will not happen. I fly out on the redeye in the morning. Besides, my time is just as valuable as Mr. Marsh's. If he doesn't value my time any more than this, he won't if I am an employee. I don't need to work under those conditions. Thank you for waking me." Ashley walks quickly toward the elevator, still refusing to look at the man.

After pushing the building's lobby button, Ashley pulls out her phone and orders a vehicle from a rideshare company. The app states the car will arrive in ten minutes. Fortunately, the vehicle comes in five, so Ashley is back in her hotel room in twenty minutes. Too angry and frustrated to be around people, Ashley throws her tote on the sofa and orders room service. She is told it will take thirty minutes. "Thirty minutes for my favorite comfort food: chips, queso, and guacamole. That figures," she says aloud to the empty hotel room.

Ashley rummages through her suitcase, finding the t-shirt and leggings she packed. Then, pulling her suit and blouse off, she stands in front of the full-length mirror and surveys her body. I'm twenty pounds heavier than I should be, but she thinks I have curves in all the right places. No one notices anyway, and it doesn't matter. Men are the least of my concern. Ashley wads the suit and blouse into a ball, tossing it into the suitcase. She quickly dons the t-shirt and leggings before sitting on the sofa with the remote, waiting for her food.

Ashley pulls her laptop out of her tote when she finds nothing that interests her on TV. Then, finally, her food arrives, and she settles in to eat and watch new videos about sustainability. After graduating with degrees in Mechanical Engineering and Architecture, Ashley focused on her love of planning and constructing buildings devoted to sustainability. And she has been very successful at it.

First, Ashley landed a position with a prestigious architectural firm in Las Vegas. She was the firm's sole architect, focusing on sustainability, and Vegas was ripe. In her five years with the firm, Ashley had designed and oversaw the construction of public school buildings and a 700-room hotel. Currently, her clients are a housing development comprising 500 apartments for seniors, another hotel and a university building. Ashley had won several awards for her work and was well known in the Las Vegas region.

But after five years, Ashley wanted more challenges. That was why she applied for a position with Marsh Architects Inc. in Los Angeles. Then, Mr. Jarod Marsh, the principal architect for the firm, stood her up. So at twenty-six years of age, Ashley will return to Vegas and her current clients. She will devote all her time and energy to them until another opportunity arises.

At 11:00, Ashley isn't the least bit sleepy after her two-hour nap on the sofa outside Mr. Marsh's office. However, she must be downstairs to catch the hotel shuttle to the airport at 3:30 am, so Ashley sets her alarm for 2:30 and climbs into bed, falling asleep quickly.

Ashley hits the snooze button twice before dragging her tired butt out of bed. She showers quickly and dresses in the work clothes she brought. Her 8:00 am meeting is at a construction site. Ashley draws her long black hair into a bun and heads downstairs. She grabs a pastry and coffee from the front desk and climbs into the shuttle.

The flight to Vegas isn't very long, but Ashley takes a nap and wakes up feeling refreshed. By the time she reaches her car in the short-term parking lot, it is 7:15. Thank goodness I planned, and everything I need for the meeting is in the car, she thinks. Unfortunately, getting to the job site will take at least thirty minutes.

The meeting at the job site takes most of the day, so Ashley decides to skip the office and go home. However, before leaving the job site, she pulls her wadded-up suit and blouse out of the suitcase to drop them off at the dry cleaners. She won't need the suit any time soon because she has others, but this one is her favorite, and it hugs her body.

Ashley's next two weeks are full of meetings and working with fellow architects on bid presentations. Luckily, there have been few problems at the job sites because Ashley is a hands-on professional. That's the way she wants it. No men or social life to interrupt her work.

At the beginning of the third week, Wesley, Ashley's boss, calls her. "Ashley, we have a new client that I am assigning to you. It will be a new challenge for you, and I think you'll enjoy it. I have scheduled a meeting for Wednesday at 1:00 pm."

"Sounds good, Wesley. I have an on-site meeting that morning, but my afternoon is free. So I'll see you then," Ashley says.

Chapter 2

JEREMY

As Jeremy boards his dad's private jet, it is a warm mid-April morning in Los Angeles. He started to fly his plane to Las Vegas but opted for the old man's jet because he is traveling on the old man's business. Besides, it will give him time to study the architect's resume he is to meet.

I should have lied to the old man and told him I was busy, so I wouldn't have to do this. My portfolio of photographs is the only thing I know about building anything. I finished my contract with the three magazines and two cities in Mexico, so I have nothing to do. Besides, I didn't have time to get up to the ranch this winter, so I missed the ski season. At least I'll get to see Wesley. It's been a long time since we've actually seen each other.

Jeremy settles into his seat and buckles his belt as the pilot says they have cleared the plane for takeoff. He opens his messenger bag, removes the resume file, and begins reading. Jeremy isn't exactly sure what he should look at in the resume. He deliberately avoided everything related to architecture since his dad and brother are in the business. His family basically ignored him after he told them he was dropping out of college to become a professional photographer. It didn't matter that Jeremy was very successful and extremely wealthy. He didn't follow in his dad's footsteps, so he became the family's black sheep and a disappointment.

As he reads the resume, Jeremy is surprised to learn that the architect the old man chose for his project is a woman, and a young woman at that. The old man has always frowned on women architects. He forbade Jeremy's older sister from becoming one, even though that was what his sister wanted to do. However, the deeper into the resume Jeremy gets, the more he is impressed with the woman's sustainability knowledge and the projects she has designed and built. He reads over the award she's won and quickly decides the old man knew what he was doing when selecting the woman for his pet project.

When the jet lands, Jeremy is pleased to find Wesley on the tarmac waiting for him. The two men went to college together for two years, but became lifelong friends and stayed in touch. After college, Wesley moved to Las Vegas and opened his successful architectural firm.

"Jeremy! Man, it is great to see you. It's been too long," Wesley says as he pulls Jeremy into a bear hug.

"I know. I've missed you," Jeremy replies. "Let me look at you." He grabs Wesley's shoulders and spins him around. "Looks like marriage agrees with you."

"Yeah, it does, but look at you, all muscular and tanned. I'm surprised you didn't bring a harem of women with you."

Jeremy laughs heartily. "I might have if I wasn't here on the old man's business."

"How did you get roped into this, anyway?"

"I finished all my contracts and had nothing to do," Jeremy replies.

"Did the ocean dry up because you usually spend summers traveling around surfing?" Wesley asks.

"Not this time. Besides, I haven't been to the ranch or seen my grandmother. So let's get lunch before I meet this superstar of yours."

Wesley grins. "She's a superstar alright, but all business. She's a loner, so don't get any ideas."

After a long lunch, Jeremy and Wesley arrive at the high-rise professional building where Wesley's firm occupies the top floor.

"Wesley, Ashley called. Unfortunately, she's running about ten minutes late," Wesley's assistant says as he and Jeremy walk into his office suite.

"That's fine. Just send her in when she gets here. Agnes, this is Jeremy Marsh. He is a new client, and Ashley will oversee his project." Agnes shakes Jeremy's offered hand. Then the two men enter Wesley's office. They chat for a few minutes by the window overlooking downtown Las Vegas.

"Jeremy, I need to go down the hall for a minute. There's coffee over in the corner if you want a cup. I'll be right back." Jeremy nods and heads to the far corner for coffee as Wesley leaves the office, leaving the door open.

Suddenly, a woman enters the office and stands in front of Wesley's desk. Jeremy can tell she doesn't know he's there, so he takes the time to look her over from bottom to top. She is wearing a pair of faded denim jeans over steel-toed boots. There are splotches of mud on the jeans. A faded denim shirt with the sleeves rolled up to her elbows is tucked inside the waistband of her jeans. Jeremy can't see her hair because it is under a white hard hat, nor can he see her face. However, Jeremy can see that the woman is very curvy in all the right places. She is not a skinny woman like the ones he constantly sees on the beaches. Damn, he thinks, I have never seen a woman look so sexy fully dressed.

Jeremy watches as the woman walks toward the windows overlooking the city. He holds his breath, waiting to see what she does next. Then the woman reaches up to her head with both hands. One hand removes the hard hat. Then the other removes the scrunchie, releasing her jet-black hair. She tosses her head from side to side, freeing her long locks, which fall across her shoulders and down her back. It is clear to Jermey the woman does not know how sexy she looks. The woman walks back to Wesley's desk and sits the hard hat on the corner just as Wesley walks in.

"Hi, Ashley. Glad you could make it," Wesley greets her.

"I'm sorry I'm late. Unfortunately, there was a problem at the job site, and I couldn't leave." The voice sounds vaguely familiar to Jeremy, and he steps out of the shadows.

"Ashley, I would like you to meet Jeremy Marsh. Jeremy, this is Ashley Winslow, our architect," Wesley says as the woman turns toward Jeremy.

Jeremy offers his hand and looks directly into the woman's face for the first time. Oh, my gosh. It's the woman that was asleep on Jarod's sofa, waiting for her interview. He shakes his head and says, "hello, Ashley. It's a pleasure to meet you."

The woman shakes his hand but continues to look downward. "Nice to meet you, too."

"Ashley, Jeremy is an old friend from college. He will be your contact for his father's project in Wyoming that I have assigned to you. I'll let Jeremy tell you about it." Ashley nods, continuing to keep her eyes downcast. "You can meet in the conference room or your office, Ashley. It's your choice. Ashley, although this is work, I doubt you have ever been to Wyoming. I want to see the area's beauty, including Yellowstone and the Grand Tetons."

"I assume by that you mean I will travel to Wyoming several times," Ashley replies.

"Based on the project Jeremy and I discussed, I believe you will spend a lot of time there. If you will pardon me, I have an appointment I need to attend. So, Jeremy, Ashley will take good care of you. I'll see you at dinner. Jennifer can't wait to see you again."

"Thanks, Wesley. I'll see you at 7:00. Ashley, please lead the way to wherever you wish to meet," Jeremy says, holding his hand for Ashley to lead the way.

Chapter 3

JEREMY

Ashley leads Jeremy to her office, ushering him inside. Jeremy walks directly over to her models of the construction projects.

"Are these your current projects?" he asks, inspecting the models closer.

"Yes," Ashley replies, walking behind her desk and sitting. She leans back in her chair and folds her arms over her chest.

"Very nice," Jeremy says, looking over his shoulder at Ashley, who refuses to look at him. "You don't remember me, do you?" he asks as he walks over to sit in a chair before the desk.

"No, should I?"

Jeremy smirks. "I believe you were asleep on my brother's sofa waiting for an interview."

"Oh, my gosh! It was you that woke me up?" Ashley asks. Jeremy nods. "You didn't tell Wesley, did you?"

"No, I said nothing to Wesley." Jeremy studies Ashley, which is relatively easy since she won't look at him.

"Well, thanks, Mr. Marsh. I didn't tell him about the interview."

"Let's get some things out of the way before we talk business," Jeremy says firmly. "You and I will work together, probably for an extended time, considering the project. I suggest you call me Jeremy." Ashley nods. "You don't trust people, especially men. Am I right, Ashley?"

Ashley raises her eyes and looks directly at Jeremy for the first time. "Why do you assume that?" she asks in a heated voice, leaning forward in her chair.

"In my line of work, it is crucial for me to read body language. You refuse to look at Wesley or me. Instead, you placed yourself behind your desk, creating a wall between us, arms crossed over your chest. That's just the beginning. There's more, but I won't waste our time discussing it further."

Ashley's jaw drops, and she grips the arms of her chair. Her blue eyes darken in anger. "Jeremy, how dare you presume to know me and what I think or feel? Perhaps you should leave and ask Wesley to find another architect for your project."

"I'm not going anywhere, Ashley, and I presumed nothing. First, my old man wants you on this project. I read your resume on the flight here, and I have to agree that you are the best suited for his so-called dream project. Second, you are going to have to learn to trust me. I would never intentionally hurt you."

"But you will," Ashley whispers, looking down at her desk.

"How do you know that?" Jeremy asks.

"Because you are a man, and that's what men do."

Jeremy feels his face turn red in anger, and he looks away from Ashley. "Shall we get started discussing the project?"

"Okay."

"My grandmother owns a vast ranch outside Jackson, Wyoming. She has a three bedroom, two-bath house there. My old man assumes she will leave the ranch to him when she dies. But, as usual, my father is getting ahead of himself. He wants to build an enormous home on the ranch. He wants it to be big enough that the entire family can spend time there together. That includes me and my siblings' families."

"That sounds like a huge house," Ashley comments.

Jeremy nods. "Since the winters are cold and there's a huge amount of snow each year, the old man also wants a game room and space to entertain guests."

"Where do I fit in?" Ashley asks curiously.

"The old man wants it to be as self-sufficient as possible. He wants it to be a showpiece designed by the superstar Ashley Winslow. Since you have never worked in a snow-covered wilderness like that, it can and will be a learning experience for you. It will test all your skills and education but may also open up new opportunities for you."

"I still don't understand why me," Ashley says.

"The old man wanted you and your knowledge in his firm. My brother blew the interview when he didn't show up for it. My father blew a gasket. I think this is his way of getting you into the firm through the back door."

"It sounds like a wonderful challenge. Honestly, I've been getting a little bored lately. So when do we start?"

Jeremy smiles, pleased he won Ashley over. "Right now. The first thing you need to do is to come to the ranch and tour it. How soon can you get away from here to do that?"

Chapter 4

ASHLEY

Ashley reaches for her phone and begins scanning her calendar. She tries to hide her shaking hands. "Let's see. Today is Wednesday. There are meetings that I have. I can't cancel until Tuesday afternoon. I don't know how long the tour will take, but I'm free until the following Monday at lunch."

"That's perfect. The ranch is so large I'm not sure that's enough time, but it's a start. I'll pick you up at 1:00 next Tuesday. Should I pick you up here or at your home?"

"Jeremy, I prefer to meet you somewhere." Ashley looks at him and sees him frown.

"Fine. May I have your phone number to text you the meeting location?"

Ashley nods and hands Jeremy her phone. "Here, just type it in for me, if you don't mind."

Jeremy hands her back her phone as he stands. "Pack warm clothing and plan to dress in layers. There's still snow on the ground in most places. Goodbye, Ashley."

As he turns to leave, Ashley takes the time to look at Jeremy's back. He is wearing brown military-style boots up to his ankles. His pants are a dark green and fit across his butt. Jeremy's shirt is loose-fitting but snug across broad, muscular shoulders. His dark brown hair is pulled into a man bun and is as dark as the full beard and mustache Ashley noticed earlier. "Wow!" she mutters as Jeremy crosses the door threshold and disappears.

Ashley spends the following days in meetings, ensuring her time away from the office will not burden her clients. Her nights and weekend are spent shopping for clothing for the trip. Ashley has checked the weather forecast for the area several times, planning her wardrobe. Finally, she is satisfied with her clothing selections and packs on Monday night.

Jeremy texted her the address for the meeting place earlier in the day. Ashley looked up the address in her Maps app and was shocked to see it was a private airfield large enough to accommodate small jets. But, of course, the Marsh family is extremely wealthy, so she thinks I shouldn't be surprised.

Ashley woke up early Tuesday morning, excited for her new adventure in Wyoming. Unfortunately, her morning meeting was long and tedious, and she had difficulty concentrating. Finally, Ashley could leave and drive the thirty minutes to the airport. Thankfully, traffic was light, and she arrived ten minutes early.

Since Jeremy had texted her to let him know when she arrived, Ashley took her time getting her things out of the car and waiting for him.

"Ashley! Hi!" Jeremy said when he was two rows away from her car. Ashley waved to him in response. But what happened next took Ashley's breath away. Jeremy walked right up to her and stood, almost touching her. He reached up with his right hand and softly brushed her cheek. The gesture caused Ashley to look up at Jeremy, seeing a tender smile crease the corners of his eyes.

"Uh, hi, Jeremy. I hope I'm not late," Ashley stammers, taking a step back.

"No, you're right on time. Let's get your stuff loaded on the plane." Jeremy grabs Ashley's suitcase and overnight bag, leaving her with her tote. She follows Jeremy through the small terminal and onto the tarmac, where a jet awaits. Next to the plane stands a man dressed in slacks with a shirt and tie. "Bill, let's get these on the plane so we can go," Jeremy shouts over the engine noise. Bill walks over, taking the bags from Jeremy. Jeremy reaches for Ashley's tote, leads her up the stairs, and onto the plane.

"Ashley, make yourself at home. Here is a coffee pot, fridge and snacks." Jeremy points to the right. "In the back is a bed and the lavatory if you want to nap. We should be in Jackson in approximately ninety minutes."

"Okay. Where are you sitting?" Ashley asks.

"Up front with the co-pilot."

"You're flying the plane?"

"Yep. My plane and I fly it most of the time. Relax, Ashley. I've been flying for years," Jeremy says with a massive grin as he wipes her lip with his fingertips. "Buckle up, and let's go to Wyoming." He turns, closes the door on the plane, and heads to the front.

"Oh wow," Ashley says as she looks around the plane, trying to decide where to sit. Finally, she selects a window seat and buckles her belt. She can hear Jeremy talking on the radio as she does.

"Ashley, we cleared for takeoff," Jeremy states, and the plane moves toward a runway.

Ashley packed a book in her tote for the flight but is too excited to read. So instead, she looks out the window during the flight, getting out of her seat once to retrieve a soft drink from the fridge. Jeremy leaves the cockpit once to check on her and make coffee for himself and the co-pilot.

Finally, the plane lands and parks beside a hanger where a four-wheel-drive vehicle waits. Once the engine stops, Jeremy opens the door and assists Ashley down the steps. Bill loads the luggage into the SUV, waves, and heads back to the plane.

Jeremy opens the door for Ashley and says, "how was your flight?"

"It was great. Thanks." Jeremy smiles, brushes Ashley's cheek and closes her door. Once in the driver's seat, Jeremy starts the vehicle and turns toward her. "It's about a forty-five-minute drive. I should have asked you if you needed to use the restroom."

"I'm good, Jeremy. I'm just excited about seeing the ranch. Does your grandmother still live there?"

"Yes, but she's in Florida now, visiting her sister. She should be back next month. There is a cook and housekeeper at the house. They are married and live in a nearby cabin. The ranch is working, so you'll see several cowboys and probably meet most of them during your stays. I have informed them of your visit and will be happy to help. By the way, we will have to share a bathroom. I hope that's not a problem."

"No, I'm fine with it. I require little in the way of comfort, Jeremy. Wow! Real cowboys?"

"Yes, and they ride actual horses to herd real cattle," Jeremy answers with a smile. He reaches over and touches Ashley's cheek again. "Okay. Now, I'll stop talking and let you enjoy the scenery unless you have questions."

Ashley turns her head away from him and looks out the window. "Why do you do that?"

"Do what?"

"Touch my cheek?"

"Mainly because I want to," Jeremy answers thoughtfully.

"Jeremy, I'm not the kind of woman you're used to," Ashley states, still looking out the window.

"I already figured that out, but you're still a beautiful woman, and I want us to be friends." He notices Ashley shakes her head slightly, but never looks at him. The ride to the house is silent, each thinking their own thoughts.

Chapter 5

JEREMY

Once they reach the house, Jeremy is pleased to see the cook and house-keeper waiting for the pair on the porch. After Jeremy introduces them to Ashley, he gives her a quick tour of the house before leading her to her bedroom.

"Jeremy, this room is so large, and the windows have a spectacular view of the mountains."

"I know. Other than the living area, your bedroom, and mine are my favorite rooms in the house. Your luggage is here, so I'll leave you alone to unpack. I'm going to do the same. It is a jack-and-jill bathroom, and the doors are open, so if you need anything, just say so. Dinner is at 6:00. Are you hungry now?"

"No, I'm good. Is it okay to wander around the house when I'm finished?" Ashley inquires.

Jeremy walks over and stands in front of her. "Of course. Ashley, this will be your home away from home during the project." He brushes her cheek and walks away quickly.

After passing through the bathroom, Jeremy sits on his bed and looks out the windows, thinking. Ashley's skin is so soft, and her lips are perfect, but she is different. Very different. I want to be her friend. I get the feeling she doesn't have any. Whether she wants to admit it to me, I'm right about her not trusting anyone. This is going to be interesting.

Jeremy hears a noise and looks toward the bathroom. Ashley is in there unpacking her personal items. She quietly closes the door on his side for a few minutes. Jeremy unpacks his things. He brought more clothes than usual because this will be his home base for several months. The housekeeper told him the boxes he had shipped to the house had been delivered. They are stored in the garage. He will only need to pack for his visits to Vegas, which he intends to be weekly.

By the time Jeremy finishes unpacking, his bathroom door is open. No sound comes from Ashley's room. He carries his items into the bathroom, shocked at the few things Ashley left. There is vanilla-scented shampoo, body wash, and a scrubby in the shower. A few basic cosmetics are sitting next to her sink.

Since I'm being nosy, Jeremy thinks, I'll also check out the medicine cabinet. Ashley placed a bottle of ibuprofen, a prescription, and deodorant in the cabinet. Also, Jeremy recognizes a pink container of pills as birth control pills. That's it. That's all Ashley left in the bathroom. She said she required a little, but this is crazy. Every female bathroom I've ever been in left absolutely no room for my stuff. Jeremy shakes his head in astonishment and heads out into the living area.

It is 5:00, and the sun is about to set. Jeremy sees Ashley standing on the back deck, watching the sun over the mountains. She is only wearing a sweatshirt and has her arms wrapped around her. He grabs a throw from the back of the sofa, walks out to the deck, and drapes it over Ashley's shoulders, careful not to touch her.

"Thank you, Jeremy," Ashley says softly. "Isn't the sunset gorgeous?"

"Yes, and the sunrise is just as spectacular. I'll make sure you see it on this trip. I'm going to have a drink. Would you like a glass of wine or something?"

"No, thank you, but you go ahead. I think I'll just sit over here and watch the sunset." Ashley sits on a chair closest to the edge of the deck to have an unobstructed view.

Jeremy walks back inside and heads over to the bar, where he pours two fingers of bourbon and watches Ashley.

"She's different, isn't she, Mr. Jeremy?" Hank, the cook, asks as he sets the table.

"Yes, Hank. She is in so many ways."

"She's beautiful and yet naïve. I'd hate to see her get hurt."

"Is that a warning, Hank?"

"No, sir. Just an observation. You aren't the only single man on this ranch, you know. I understand she will be here off and on for a while, which means she will be around the men and, as beautiful as she is, they will go out of their way to be around her," Hank says.

"I'll just have to keep an eye on her."

"Mr. Jeremy, you're a man with your own needs to satisfy in town. That is, unless you've turned into a saint, which I doubt. Your name and reputation precede you around here. Women have already been calling asking if you've arrived yet."

Jeremy turns his eyes away from Ashley and looks at Hank. "Really?" Jeremy asks, his eyes twinkling. Hank nods. "Well, I haven't been here in a long time, so I bet there is an abundance of new prospects just waiting for me."

"And some of the old ones. It's not every day Jeremy Marsh, award-winning photographer, skier, surfer and mountain climber, comes for a visit. I think you'll be too busy to worry about Miss Ashley. I bet Tyler will be the first to meet her."

Jeremy rolls his eyes at Hank. "Tyler?"

"Oh yeah, he's become quite a lady's man since he got promoted to ranch foreperson and has more free time to go into town and hang out. So he's probably warmed several women up for you. Actually, he invited himself to dinner tonight to meet Ashley."

"Crap!" Jeremy says, bringing his fist down hard on the top of the bar. Just then, Tyler approaches the deck and Ashley.

Chapter 6

ASHLEY

A shley shivers and pulls the throw Jeremy brought her tighter around her arms. The sunset over the mountains mesmerized her. Never has she seen anything so vivid and in the natural colors of a wilderness. But now, it is getting dark, and dinner's aroma teases her nose. Suddenly, the clearing of a throat breaks the silence of the early evening. Ashley turns her head toward the sound.

"Good evening. I hope I didn't scare you," a tall, muscular man asks from the side of the deck.

"No, I just wasn't expecting anyone," Ashley says, standing.

"I'm Tyler, the ranch foreperson," the man says, reaching out his hand. "You must be Ashley. It's a genuine pleasure to meet you."

Ashley looks down at his hand and cautiously accepts it just as the door to the house opens.

"Tyler," Jeremy says.

"Hi, Jeremy. Welcome back. I know there are a lot of women in town just waiting to meet you or see you again."

"Excuse me," Ashley says. "I'll wash up for dinner and leave you two to talk." She quickly leaves the deck and the men behind. She walks into her bedroom laughing. "Well, that was interesting. Like two male dogs making their territory," Ashley says aloud.

Dinner is pleasant, except at the beginning when Jeremy announces Hank and Ida will join them for dinner. When Tyler comments it is unusual, Jeremy replies, well, you're here, aren't you? Ashley notices Hank and Ida exchange looks at the comment.

They gear most of the conversation toward the ranch and its operations. If questions are asked about Ashley, she deflects the conversation by asking about the ranch. Finally, Tyler excuses himself, stating he has an early morning to prepare for.

"Ashley, would you like to watch TV, play cards or something?" Jeremy asks, rising from his chair.

"Cards sound like fun, but I'm afraid you will have to teach me," Ashley replies, embarrassed.

"I would be happy to," Jeremy replies. "What sounds good to you? Hearts, spades, poker, rummy?"

"Anything. You pick. Hank, can I help you clean up?"

"Miss Ashley, thank you, but no. Ida helps me." Ashley nods and follows Jeremy to the living area, where Jeremy is fumbling around in a desk drawer.

"Oh, a fireplace with natural wood. I've never been around one before, although I've designed several natural gas and electric ones," Ashley comments.

Jeremy looks at her over his shoulder. "Grab that throw you had on earlier and come with me," he tells her. Ashley does as instructed and follows Jeremy out the front door. He stands still momentarily and then grabs her hand. Ashley starts to pull it away, but Jeremy holds on tightly. Finally, he leads her to the side of the house. "Now, take a deep breath," he says, releasing her hand.

Ashley breathes deeply while Jeremy watches her. She smiles but doesn't look at him. "So that's what wood smoke smells like. It is wonderful, Jeremy. Thank you."

Chapter 7

JEREMY

Jeremy stares at Ashley in the darkness. She's never been around a wood fire or smelled the smoke from one. Yet, she's an accomplished architect. This woman is strange, but I found myself enjoying her company. He watches as Ashley moves slightly to see the smoke from the fireplace rise in the sky in the moonlight.

Suddenly, Ashley lies down on the ground looking up. "Jeremy, look at all the stars. The sky is so clear."

He shakes his head and lies down beside her. "If you think this is nice, I'll take you to a place where you can see much more."

"Oh, Jeremy. I would love that. Can you see the milky way from there?"

"Probably. I'll check the weather for tomorrow night. Maybe we can do it then." He thinks I just committed to spending tomorrow night with Ashley. I was planning to go to Jackson and see some friends. She'll get cold quickly, so maybe I can go afterward. After several minutes, Jeremy says, "let's go inside. I bet you're getting cold."

"Okay," Ashley replies, ignoring Jeremy's outstretched hand.

Once inside the house, Ashley says, "I think I'll turn in. It's been a long and exciting day. Good night Jeremy."

"Sleep well, Ashley," he replies, touching her cheek.

Unready to go to bed, Jeremy pours himself a bourbon and leans back on the sofa. There are many things he takes for granted that Ashley finds joy in. But, *perhaps I've been away from here too long.*

The house is tranquil, so when Jeremy hears a tiny sound, he wakes up immediately. He lies in bed, trying to determine the sound's origin. The sound grows slightly louder and sounds like a wounded animal whimpering. Jeremy climbs out of bed and walks toward the bathroom. The sound is coming from Ashley's room. Silently, he walks into her room, where he sees Ashley uncovered and curled in a fetal position in the center of the bed. She is whimpering and shaking. He hurries over to the side of the bed.

Afraid of startling her, Jeremy leans over and whispers, "Ashley. Ashley, wake up, baby." She doesn't wake. He gently touches her shoulder. "Ashley, baby. Wake up."

Still, she doesn't wake. Jeremy watches as the whimpering and shaking continue. Unsure of what he should do, Jeremy does the only thing he knows. He climbs into bed and gets as close to Ashley's back as possible. Jeremy lays his arm over her after covering them both. After several minutes, the whimpering and shaking stop. Jeremy feels Ashley's body relax, and she straightens out her legs and falls into a peaceful sleep.

The chirping of a bird outside wakes Jeremy. For a moment, he's confused about where he is. Then, lying on his side, he looks over at Ashley and remembers he's in her bed and why he's there. She is snuggling up against him, breathing softly. Jeremy carefully untangles himself from her body and climbs out of bed, heading toward the bathroom.

After silently closing the door, he turns the shower on. As the water heats, Jeremy recalls last night and wonders what happened in Ashley's life that caused her to have such a horrible dream. Tears come to his eyes as he replays her whimpering and position. *Hopefully, she won't remember the night,* Jeremy thinks. Ashley may be embarrassed and retreat farther into herself just when she seems to loosen up a little.

After showering and dressing, Jeremy heads to the kitchen, where Hank is waiting with a pot of coffee. "Mr. Jeremy, you look terrible. Did you not sleep well?"

"Ashley had a bad dream last night that I hope she won't remember. I couldn't wake her, and I only knew to hold her until she calmed down."

"Jeremy, tell us about the dream," Ida says, walking into the room.

"I can't tell you about the dream, but Ashley was whimpering, shaking, and lying in a fetal position. Then, after I held her for a little while, she calmed down, straightened out her body, and fell into a deep sleep." Jeremy sees Ida and Hank exchange looks, and Ida nods her head. "What?"

"Mr. Jeremy, you didn't ask, but I will give you my opinion based on what I've seen of Miss Ashley and what you just said. She was abused as a child."

Jeremy looks at Hank and then at Ida. "Why would you say that?"

"My sister was the same way. Our father was a mean drunk. He beat our mother and us constantly. I was older and tried to protect my sister, but usually, I was beaten first and couldn't help her. She trusted no one but me and retreated into herself, plagued by bad dreams and nightmares."

"Where's your sister now?" Jeremy asks.

"She purposely overdosed on heroin. She left home before me and began taking drugs to ease the pain and suffering in her mind. Ida and I tried to help her, but it was no use. She did the only thing she knew to do to find peace," Hank says.

"Surely not. Ashley's a little strange, but surely she wasn't abused," Jeremy states.

"Jeremy, she doesn't trust anyone. She refuses to look at anyone directly and always deflects questions about herself. As a result, I believe you may witness more nightmares," Ida states.

"Good morning, everyone," Ashley says, walking into the kitchen looking just as bad as Jeremy. "Is that coffee I smell because I could use an extra large cup?"

Hank laughs and hands her a hot cup. "Well, what do you two have planned for the day?"

"I thought I would ask you to pack us lunch, and I will take Ashley on a tour of the ranch," Jeremy replies, looking at Ashley. "The best way to see the ranch is on horseback, but we'll take the four-wheeler instead." He winks at Ashley.

"Thank goodness," Ashley says with a grin.

Jeremy's phone rings. "Excuse me. I need to take this." He steps into the adjoining room and answers. "Hi, G. How are you? Okay. Great. Text me the time, and I'll pick you up. Love you too. Bye."

"That was G, my grandmother," he tells the group. "She's coming home tomorrow. I'll pick her up at the airport."

"Jeremy, would you mind if I ride along? I must visit a few places to get information on the area." Ashley asks.

"I don't mind at all. I'll enjoy the company, and you'll get to meet G. She's looking forward to meeting you."

Chapter 8

ASHLEY

Jeremy and Ashley leave the house after breakfast and head east. Jeremy takes Ashley to his favorite spot on the ranch, on the side of a mountain. From that location, the pair can see the valley below, where some cowboys are herding cattle.

"What are they doing?" Ashley asks.

"The cattle have spent the winter in the valley, so it's time to move them into the hills where the new grass grows. They will graze in the hills until fall and then be moved back here. Some will be rounded up to sell, and others will stay until next spring. Many of the cows are pregnant and will give birth either on the way to the hills or when they get there," Jeremy answers, pointing at the herd.

Tyler is at the front of the herd. He spied Jeremy and Ashley and waves. Ashley waves back and says, "why is Tyler in front? Is it because he's the foreperson?"

Jeremy huffs. "No, some cowboys are new to the ranch. Tyler has been here a long time and knows the best way to the hills. Let's move on."

The day warms up, and Jeremy stops by a stream at lunchtime. After eating, Ashley lies on the blanket, looking up at the sky. "It is so quiet and peaceful here," she remarks. "Jeremy, tell me about yourself. You know more about me than I do you."

"Well," Jeremy says, lying down beside her. "My old man thought I should be an architect too and sent me to college. That's where I met Wesley. After two years, I decided an architect was the last thing I wanted to be. So I quit college and went to a trade school to learn photography. My old man was furious and refused to pay for my classes. So G helped me, and I worked part-time at a pizza place." Jeremy stops for a few seconds before continuing. "I decided to start a photography business, and G loaned me the money. I have been fortunate to land contracts with governments, cities, magazines and other companies. With these contracts, I've traveled all over the world. That's one reason I have my own jet. It's easier and cheaper than flying commercially."

"Wow! I'm impressed," Ashley says. "I had no idea. What do you do for fun?"

Jeremy laughs. "I'm into extreme sports; I guess you could say. I do all types of skiing in winter. During the summer, I enjoy surfing and mountain climbing. I can often incorporate my activities with photography depending on the contracts I get."

Ashley rises and leans on her elbow, looking at Jeremy. "No wonder you're in such good shape." Jeremy looks over at her, and she blushes.

"So, you've noticed my body?" he asks with a smirk.

Ashley rolls her eyes and lies back. "How could I not notice?"

"Well, most of the time, you won't even look at me, so I didn't know," Jeremy replies honestly.

"Oh, I look, Jeremy. Trust me, I look. Shall we go? I have a feeling there's a lot more ranch to see." Ashley sits up and tries to stand, but Jeremy grabs her arm.

"Wait, Ashley. Tell me about you," he says.

"You said you read my resume. That's all there is to know about me." Ashley shakes his hand off her arm, stands, and begins gathering the picnic lunch items from the blanket.

The pair devotes the rest of the day riding around various locations on the ranch. Then, as they return to the house, Ashley points at a small building near Jeremy's favorite spot she had overlooked earlier. "What's that?" she asks.

"We call it a line shack. It is a small cabin that can sleep up to four people. Sometimes it gets too late for the cowboys to go back to the bunkhouse, or they have to take turns guarding the herd. Hank keeps it stocked with food and firewood because no one knows when they will need it," Jeremy answers.

"Can I see it?"

"I'll show it to you later when we return here so you can look at the sky."

"Oh, Jeremy. I can hardly wait," Ashley replies, blesses Jeremy with a big smile, and looks directly into his eyes.

Chapter 9

JEREMY

eremy's heart nearly stops beating when Ashley's blue eyes meet his. Even though she is grinning and is excited, he can see the sadness in her eyes. He smooths her cheek with his fingertips and says, "I'm so happy you're enjoying this. I have taken everything here for granted for so long. It's nice to see it through your eyes." Ashley blushes and looks away. "Let's go have dinner, and then we'll return."

After dinner, Ashley goes to her room to change into warmer clothes while Jeremy prepares things for their excursion to view the stars. He packs blankets, flashlights, a thermos of hot chocolate, and a rifle onto the four-wheeler. Then Jeremy rushes upstairs to change himself. He wears his hair down for a change, so his long, deep brown locks fall to his shoulders. He's curious if Ashley will notice and say anything about it.

As Ashley climbs into the vehicle, she sees the rifle. "A rifle, Jeremy?"

"Yes, for protection from the wolves if needed. I don't intend to kill any. Just scare them off. Are you ready?" Ashley giggles and nods.

Jeremy drives the vehicle to the valley where he and Ashley saw the cattle earlier in the day. While Ashley holds a flashlight, Jeremy spreads two blankets on the ground. Then he unpacks the rest of the items he packed.

"Okay, I think we're ready. Lie down," he tells Ashley. She does, and he lies beside her with his shoulder touching hers, leaving the flashlight on.

"Oh my gosh, Jeremy. This is magical," Ashley says, turning her head from the sky to look at him. "You let your hair down. It looks so soft and wavy. Can I touch it?" He nods, and she leans up on one elbow and combs her fingers through his hair.

More women than Jeremy can remember have done the same thing, but it feels different with Ashley. It feels warm and calming. She is tender, and the flashlight's light makes her eyes glow. Suddenly, her hand stops in mid-air. Her face looks confused, and she lies down on her back quickly. Jeremy turns the flashlight off.

The pair lie in silence for a long time, watching the stars. Wolves howl in the distance, making Ashley shiver.

"Do the wolves scare you?" Jeremy asks.

"No, they just sound so lonely, like I feel most of the time. I shouldn't have said that. I'm sorry."

"Don't be sorry to share your feelings with me. Everyone feels lonely sometimes. Let me show you some constellations." Jeremy points out several that are easily visible. Then he points to one that is hard to see. "Do you see it, Ashley?"

"No, I don't. Where is it?"

"Here. Let me show you." Jeremy takes her hand and points to the stars. "Now, can you see it?" Ashley shakes her head. "Lie your head on my shoulder while I point to it. Maybe then you can see it." Ashley does and follows the line of his and her outstretched hands.

"Oh, I see it now," Ashley says excitedly, but she doesn't move her head from Jeremey's shoulder. He deeply inhales the scent of her vanilla shampoo and body wash. Even though her hair tickles his nose, Jeremy refuses to move and enjoys the feel of her warmth. Ashley lies there for a while, forgetting her head is on his shoulder. Finally, Jeremy can't take the tickling feeling anymore. He reaches up and moves the lock of hair from his nose to behind her ear, brushing her cheek as he does.

"I'm sorry," Ashley says as she moves away from him, holding Jeremy's hand. "Jeremy, that looks like lightning over the mountain."

"You're right. There's supposed to be a rainstorm overnight. If I'm going to show you the line shack, we better go now. I want to get back to the house before the rain starts." Jeremy turns on the flashlight. He and Ashley quickly gather everything, pack it on the four-wheeler, and take off.

It is a short drive to the line shack. When they arrive, Jeremy drives to the back of the building and parks under an awning. "Let me start the generator so we'll have lights," he tells Ashley as he climbs off the vehicle. Once the generator runs, Jeremy helps Ashley off the four-wheeler and hands her the thermos of hot chocolate. He grabs her hand and leads her to the back door. Jeremy unlocks the door and reaches inside, turning the lights on.

"It's very rustic but comfortable when needed," Jeremy says as Ashley steps inside first. "I think we made it just in time. Unfortunately, it's starting to rain."

"Jeremy, this is great," Ashley says, looking around the cabin. "It feels like a small home."

"I'm glad you think so, because I believe we will be here until the storm blows through. I'll bring in some wood and get a fire started. Why don't you pour us some cocoa while I do?" Jeremy tells her.

After a while, the burning fire warms the cabin. Ashley and Jeremy sit at a small table, finishing the cocoa.

"Jeremy, have you ever considered living here permanently?"

"No, I never have. I have my job and a commitment in Vegas. Plus, there isn't much to do here in the way of fun after ski season."

"It sounds like you thrive taking part in dangerous sports. So what are you running from? What are you trying to prove?" Ashley asks.

"Those are weird questions. I'm not running from anything. I could ask you the same thing," Jeremy replies.

"I didn't run away. I walked, and it was a bad situation, but I don't want to discuss it. It's late. Perhaps we should get some sleep. After all, you have to pick up your grandmother at the airport tomorrow." Ashley stands and turns. "Which bed do you want?"

Jeremy shakes his head. "Will you ever trust me enough to talk to me?"

Ashley looks down at him and says, "it's not so much my trusting you. It's how much I trust myself with you, knowing that trust will cause me great pain at some point." She turns away from him and walks to a bed to her right. "I'll sleep here." Ashley turns back the bedcovers and crawls into bed, facing away from Jeremy.

Jeremy stares at her back for a long time, pondering her words. Man, this woman is so confusing, he thinks. Why am I trying to get to know her when she's constantly putting up walls between us? That's it. Tomorrow night, I'm going into town and find a woman to keep me warm with no thinking required.

Chapter 10

ASHLEY

The sound of rain on the metal roof conjures up memories, keeping Ashley awake. She listens to Jeremy's even breathing and climbs out of bed. Then, grabbing a blanket, she eases the front door of the cabin open and steps out onto the front porch. The rain is coming down in sheets. Thunder and lightning roll across the valley below the cabin.

Ashley sits in a rocking chair beside the cabin, gathering the blanket around her. She closes her eyes and remembers it was a night much like this when she saw her mother for the last time. First, her mother tucked Ashley and her baby brother into their shared bed. Then, after kissing their foreheads, her mother walked into the kitchen, only to be met by the raving lunatic, Ashley's father. First, he began the fight like he always did, calling her mother a whore. Then he started yelling Bible verses he twisted for his sick justification.

To Ashley, it seemed like every time there was a crash of thunder, something in the house broke. She could hear her mother crying, pleading for Ashley's father to stop. Just like the thunder and lightning, the storm in the house continued. But then the storm moved away, as did the storm inside the house. It was an eerie quiet that sent shivers up Ashley's spine.

"Ashley, are you okay?" The sound of Jeremy's voice and the porch light coming on stop Ashley's memories.

"Jeremy, I didn't hear you." He walks in front of her and kneels between her knees.

"You've been crying," Jeremy whispers as he wipes the tears from her cheeks. "Do you want to talk about it?" Ashley shakes her head and stares at her folded hands lying in her lap. "Come with me," he says softly, taking her hands from her lap.

Jeremy leads her into the cabin, sits on his bed, and pulls Ashley into his lap. "They say crying can soothe a troubled soul. So if you feel like crying, please do it with me holding you." Ashley sniffles and lays her face against Jeremy's neck. He wraps his arms around her as she sobs.

The sobs wrack Ashley's body and continue for over an hour. After what seems like an eternity, the sobs slow and finally end. Jeremy stands, lifting the woman and placing her on his bed. As Ashey watches, Jeremy pulls off his tear-soaked shirt and climbs into bed beside her. He pulls her into his arms and holds her tightly against him as she falls asleep.

Pink light from the sunrise peeks through the windows, waking Ashley. She opens her eyes and gazes at the handsome man sleeping beside her. Ashley softly brushes the hair from his cheek and touches his beard. She expected it to be coarse and stiff, but there is a softness to it. Carefully lifting the arm encircling her waist, Ashley slides from underneath the leg covering hers. Jeremy turns over on his back.

Standing next to the bed, she scrutinizes Jeremy, seeing him without a shirt for the first time. One large scar stretches from his shoulder to his sternum. Several smaller scars dot his six-pack abs. Dark brown hair covers the upper part of his chest and thins as it weaves toward his waist. I could fall for this handsome man, she thinks. But I'm neither his type nor worthy of such a man.

Ashley grabs her coat and quietly leaves the warmth of the cabin. The morning air is clean and crisp after the rain. The sky is clear, promising a beautiful day. Ashley carefully walks around the cabin, studying it with her methodical mind working rapidly. Using her size eight shoes, she measures the cabin's size and estimates the roof's slope. Then Ashley follows the path where the water drained off the roof. She ends up standing ten feet from the front of the cabin. A movement from the front door catches her eye.

"Coffee?" a smiling Jeremy stands in the doorway holding a steaming cup.

"Yes, please," Ashley replies. She bends over and removes her boots when she reaches the porch.

"Let me," Jeremy says. He hands her the cup of coffee and motions for her to sit. When she does, he unties the laces and removes the muddy boots. Then he offers a hand to help her stand. Ashley takes his hand and stands. Jeremy moves closer, leans in, and gently kisses her cheek.

"Jeremy, thank you for taking care of me last night." Ashley looks into his dark brown eyes.

"We all need a good cry occasionally." He brushes a lock of her hair behind her ear.

"Even you?"

"Even me," Jeremy answers. Ashley sees the pain in his eyes before he looks down and turns away. "I was serious, Ashley. If you want to cry, I want you to do it while I hold you. It makes me feel you need me. Now, let's pack up and get to the house," he says, changing the subject quickly. "I need to pick up my grandmother at lunch. Do you still want to ride into town with me?"

"No, I decided what I need will come from Cheyenne, and I'll order it online. Jeremy, would your grandmother let me use the line shack for a test site?"

"I'm sure she would, but you can ask her yourself over dinner tonight. Are you sure you don't want to go with me?" Jeremy asks, almost sounding hurt.

"Yes, I've taken up far too much of your time. You need time for yourself and with friends. I don't need you to entertain or babysit me." Ashley stands in front of Jeremy, touches his cheek, and smiles. "I enjoy your company greatly, and you are there when I need you, even if you don't know it. I do," she whispers.

Chapter 11

JEREMY

As soon as he pulls out of the driveway to go to the airport, Jeremy realizes he already misses Ashley. The road is slick in some areas from last night's rain. Also, a few boulders in the roadway must be dodged, so he is forced to pay attention to driving, not Ashley.

Jeremy's phone rings a few miles outside of town. It is a long-time friend inviting Jeremy out tonight for a night of drinking, dancing, and womanizing. Jeremy agrees immediately. They agree to meet at a popular bar outside the city limits at 7:30. Jeremy decides this will be just what I need to clear my head.

The plane from Florida is delayed an hour. Jeremy drives to the hangar and checks on his jet in the meantime. After all, today is Thursday, and he must take Ashley back to Vegas on Sunday. Then Jeremy quickly calls his usual hotel to ensure a room is available for him Sunday through Friday. He'll come back to the ranch on Friday, hopefully with Ashley.

Jeremy waits for his grandmother in the baggage claim area of the terminal. He knows she did lots of shopping while in Florida with her sister. He sees the older, petite woman first and trots toward her. She screams his name and jumps into his arms when they meet.

"Jeremy, my dearest love! It is wonderful to see you. I've missed you so much."

"G, it's about time you came home. The kids and I have missed you so much. Little Timmy has been crying for his mother for a week. How many suitcases did you bring home with you? Did you max out our credit card?" Jeremy asks, carrying her like a bride over a threshold toward the luggage carousel.

"I think you can put me down now," G whispers. "That should give everyone here something to talk about for several days."

Jeremy laughs and sets her down on the floor. "Well, you look young enough to be my wife."

G elbows him in the ribs. "You better go get a cart. You can't carry everything." Jeremy does as he's told. When he returns, G has eight suitcases sitting on the floor waiting for him. Jeremy raises his eyebrows in disbelief. "I needed new linens and things," G says sheepishly.

Once in the car, G demands Jeremy tell her everything from the beginning. She knows something important brought him back to the ranch.

"It's going to take longer than forty-five minutes, so we better stop for lunch," Jeremy says.

G laughs. "I agree. Those snacks on the plane didn't last long, even though I asked for an extra bag."

Once seated and their orders placed, Jeremy and G get down to business. He starts at the beginning with his contracts ending, being summoned to his father's office, and finishes with his father's plan for the monster house on the ranch.

G listens intently and rarely interrupts. Finally, when Jeremy finishes, G looks him in the eyes and says, "now tell me about Ashley."

"There's nothing to tell, G. She is a talented architect." Jeremy looks down at his plate.

"Jeremy Marsh, don't sit there and give me that BS. Hank and Ida said she seems like a very nice young woman with some issues. I can see you like her. Now talk to me."

"You should have been a police detective, G. Okay, here goes." Jeremy starts at the beginning, when he first finds Ashley on Jarod's sofa. He talks about her nightmares, trust issues, childlike enthusiasm and wonder at the ranch property, and how she takes everything in stride without complaining.

"You like her," G states.

Jeremy rolls his eyes. "I like her because she's unlike any woman I've ever known. Ashley accepts me for me. She did not know I was rich and had won many awards for skiing, surfing and photography. She could have searched the internet and found out about me, but she didn't."

"Maybe that's a good thing. But she would have also learned what a womanizer you are. That would have terrified her if she always had trust issues. If you're finished eating, let's head home. I'm tired, and we must discuss your father's grand plans."

"Where's Ashley?" Jeremy asks Hank when he and G get home.

"She's at the line shack. She said she needed to think about her plans before she talks to G," Hank answers.

"What plans?" G asks, looking at Jeremy.

"She'll have to tell you. I do not know. Hank, is she there by herself?"

"I don't think so, Mr. Jeremy. I saw Tyler headed that direction when Ashley was halfway there."

"Crap," Jeremy says, running out of the house toward the line shack.

Chapter 12

ASHLEY

I fully intended to be here alone and think, but no, Tyler shows up, Ashley thinks to herself as she looks out the window. Why did I leave the door open?

"Hello, Miss Ashley. I saw you come this way and wondered if I could assist." Tyler crosses the threshold and walks into the cabin.

"Hi, Tyler. No, thank you. I just wanted to work out a few details on a proposal for Jeremy's grandmother."

"Are you sure?" Ashley nods. "Well, why don't I make us some coffee, and we can get to know each other?" Tyler moves closer to Ashley, making her feel uneasy.

"I don't think so, Tyler. I have little time and want to discuss it with her over dinner." Ashley turns and moves to the opposite side of the table, trying to distance herself and Tyler. However, Tyler grabs her arm.

"Ashley, you're a beautiful woman. I'm available to help you in any way possible," Tyler smirks.

"Tyler, I suggest you let go of me and never touch me again. If I want your help, I'll ask for it," Ashley says, trying to pull her arm away without success.

"The lady told you to let go of her, Tyler," Jeremy growls, stepping into the cabin.

Tyler immediately drops his hand from Ashley's arm. "Well, look who's here. Jeremy, Ashley, and I were chatting and getting to know each other a little before you barged in."

Ashley watches the exchange between the two men. She can see the fire in Jeremy's dark brown eyes as he stares at Tyler.

"Get lost, Tyler," Jeremy demands.

"Okay, okay. Ashley, I'll be at the bunkhouse whenever you need a real man's help or if Jeremy is out too busy womanizing at the local bars." Tyler walks past Jeremy and out the door.

"Ashley, are you okay?" Jeremy asks, hurrying over to her. She nods. "Let me see your arm." She holds it out to him. Jeremy takes it, pushes up her sleeve, and inspects her arm. "Your skin is so fair and soft. I think you might have a bruise or two." Jeremy holds her arm, but brushes her cheek with his free hand. He looks up, and Ashley is staring at him.

"What did Tyler mean about you womanizing at the local bars?" she asks softly.

"It's not important," Jeremy says, looking down and releasing Ashley's arm. "Tyler was just making a comment."

Ashley backs away and walks out the door. "I'm finished, so you can lock up on your way out." By the time Jeremy reaches the door, Ashley has run halfway to the house.

Back in her bedroom, Ashley grabs her laptop, logging into the internet. She searches Jeremy's name and finds almost non-stop photos of Jeremy with beautiful blond women. Most could be models, and some probably are, she determines. There are images of Jeremy and the women on the beach, on the ski slopes, at dinners, dances, and on and on and on. Ashley searches for Jeremy and serious relationships, finding none. Some are mentioned that lasted a few weeks or months, but that's all. So that's what Tyler meant about womanizing, Ashley decides.

A knock on her door interrupts Ashley's thoughts. "Dinner's served," Ida tells her.

"Thanks, Ida. I'm on my way. Tell everyone they can start without me." Ashley closes her laptop, washes her hands, and heads to the dining room, where Jeremy introduces Ashley to his grandmother. The grandmother insists Ashley calls her G.

After the introductions, G sits at the head of the table with Jeremy and Ashley on each side. Ashley begins the conversation by asking about G's trip to Florida. Ashley refuses to look at Jeremy, although she constantly feels his eyes on her.

Halfway through dinner, G asks Ashley about her proposal. Ashley explains she would like to use the line shack for several tests, including a rainwater collection system. She tells G that although she can use historical data for her analysis, real-time data would benefit her research.

G listens intently and asks questions along the way. Finally, she says, "Ashley, I have to be honest and tell you hell will freeze over before I leave the ranch to that imbecile father of Jeremy's. He might be married to my daughter, but doesn't appreciate the ranch or anything about it. It has been in my family for generations. If I have to, I'll leave it to a charity or the state as a park."

"I understand," Ashley says quietly, looking down at her plate.

"I'm not finished," G says. "I want you to continue what that old fool has contracted you for. After all, you're earning and spending his money. I want you to do whatever you want with the line shack. Then, we can see what works and what doesn't. I may decide to update this house with your ideas."

"Thank you, G. I have mixed emotions about the house Mr. Marsh wants to build. A location for that size house would destroy much of the beauty of the ranch," Ashley states.

"I'm glad you feel that way," G replies.

Jeremy stands and says, "ladies, if you will excuse me, I have plans to meet some friends in town tonight. Congratulations, Ashley."

Ashley watches Jeremy walk toward the front door to grab his coat. He is wearing his soft brown hair down on his shoulders. His shirt is tight across the shoulders but hangs loosely around his waist. The tapered legs of his fitted jeans are tucked into black military-style boots. She lets out a sigh.

"He's a handsome man, don't you agree?" G says.

"I suppose if you like that kind of man."

"What kind of man, Ashley?"

"The kind that likes to push his limits and would bore easily."

"Jeremy hasn't had an easy life. It's taken a long time for him to find his place in the world. I think he's still working on that, though. Now, let's talk business. I didn't want to say this in front of Jeremy," G says.

"I can keep a secret if needed," Ashley replies.

"Great. I plan to leave the ranch to Jeremy. He'll realize his place is here and will need a home someday. Hopefully, he'll settle down with a wonderful woman and have a house full of children. I was hoping you could design a place for him you think he would like. You can do it under the guise of designing his father's stupid monstrosity."

Ashley smiles. "I can do that, and I know its location. I believe I can get Jeremy's ideas without him realizing what I'm doing."

"Fantastic. Now, I'm going to call it a night. I'm tired. I'll see you in the morning, Ashley."

"G, before you go. Is there a vehicle I can use tomorrow? I want to drive into town and check the supplies I need."

"Sure. My car is in the garage. I'll give you the keys in the morning. Goodnight, dear."

Ashley spends the evening in her bedroom making a list of needed items. She decides to start with a rainwater collection system. Someone on the ranch hauled five-gallon water bottles to the line shack. The system will free up that person's time and eliminate back fatigue. At 11:00, she crawls into bed but cannot fall asleep. Ashley wonders what Jeremy is doing and why she cares. You're jealous, a little voice inside her says. Nope, she replies. I don't care.

Ashley heads down to breakfast the following morning to find she is alone. Hank tells her G went out for a drive in the four-wheeler, and Jeremy wasn't home yet. Hank gives her the keys to G's car. Ashley leaves quickly, not wanting to be there when Jeremy gets home.

Chapter 13

JEREMY

"**W**as that Ashley I passed, driving G's car on the road?" Jeremy asks Hank when he walks into the kitchen.

"It was," Hank answers. "She wanted to run into town and see about the supplies she needs."

"I would have gone with her if she had waited."

"Not looking and smelling like that," G says, walking into the kitchen. Jeremy looks at her with a confused face. "Your clothes look like you slept in them, and you reek of a woman's perfume."

Jeremy smiles shyly. "I ran into Blair at the bar last night."

"Well, I hope you had a good time. Now, you can spend the morning figuring out what happened with Ashley," G declares.

"What do you mean?"

"She would look at you last night and avoided talking to you."

"Yeah, well, she's like that sometimes," Jeremy replies.

"I thought you said things were getting better. Find out, Jeremy, and get it corrected. She will be around for a while, and I don't want my home to feel like an indoor freezer."

Jeremy nods, grabs a cup of coffee, and goes to his bedroom. While the shower heats, he replays yesterday in his mind. Everything was fine between him and Ashley until Tyler mouthed off. A thought hits Jeremy. He goes into Ashley's room and looks around for her laptop. He sees it on the nightstand next to the bed. Hundreds of pictures of him are staring him in the face as he opens it. But not just him. All the pictures are of him and many of the blond-haired, blue eyes beauties he has surrounded himself with the last two years.

"Dammit, dammit, dammit!" Jeremy says aloud. Tyler opened a can of worms with his remark about Jeremy's womanizing. It's not that Jeremy was hiding it from Ashley, but he wanted to be the one to tell her and explain why. What difference does it make, he asks himself? Because you like her a lot and want her to trust you, his inner voice says. "Yeah, I do," Jeremy says aloud.

After washing Blair's perfume from his body, Jeremy lies down for a nap, recalling his night and morning with Blair. She had missed him and spent all night proving just how much. But Jeremy's mind was elsewhere most of the time. A beauty with raven hair and a curvaceous body was in the back of his mind the entire time. What would it be like to kiss Ashley? What would she be like in bed? Would she look at him? Would she ever trust him enough? Finally, Jeremy falls asleep, exhausted from his thoughts and sexual escapades with Blair.

Ashley and G are having lunch when Jeremy enters the dining room. "Hi, ladies," he says cheerfully. "Ashley, did you get everything you needed while in town?"

Ashley answers with her eyes on her food, "most of it. I had to order a few things. Is it possible to take me home a day early?"

"I suppose. Is it necessary?" Jeremy asks.

"Yes, everything will be delivered in two weeks, and I can start to work. But I must get back, make arrangements to be here for the delivery, and oversee the work."

"Is there anything Jeremy or I can do while you're gone to help?" G asks.

"I really need two or three men to help with construction. Of course, I can do the work myself, but it will go faster if I have help," Ashley replies.

"I'll ask around town," Jeremy says.

"And I'll ask the cowboys if they have any experience in construction. We'll make sure you have the help you need, Ashley."

"So, what time would you like to leave tomorrow?" Jeremy asks.

"As early as possible," Ashley replies, rising from the table. "Excuse me. I think I'll take a walk and enjoy the beautiful afternoon."

Jeremy starts to follow her, but G grabs his arm and shakes her head. "Leave her alone, Jeremy." Hank comes out of the kitchen with Jeremy's lunch and sits down to eat. "Did you come up with anything?"

"Yeah, I think so," Jeremy says as he eats. "Yesterday, when Tyler was at the cabin with Ashley, he commented on my womanizing. So while she was gone this morning, I looked at her laptop. She had hundreds of pictures with me with women I dated or took to social events."

"What are you going to do about it?" G asks.

"I think when she comes back, I'll bring Devon with me and explain about the last two years," Jeremy answers.

"That sounds like a good plan. It will be nice to have Devon around. I hope your plan works."

Chapter 14

ASHLEY

Saturday morning is as gloomy as Ashley's mood. She spent all yesterday afternoon and most of the evening avoiding Jeremy. Now, she dreads the drive to the airport alone with him. But thankfully, at the last minute, G decides to tag along. That way, she can bring the SUV back instead of leaving it at the hangar for a week or so while Jeremy takes care of his business in Vegas.

The flight home is quiet, and Ashley naps. When they reach Vegas, Bill, Jeremy's co-pilot, loads Ashley's luggage into her car while Jeremy loads his own into a rental car.

"Ashley, just text me when you are ready to head back to Jackson," Jeremy says as he climbs into his car and drives off.

The first thing Ashley does when she reaches her apartment is to text Wesley, her boss, requesting a meeting early Monday morning. Then she starts her laundry and makes a shopping list for food. While her clothes are in the washer and dryer, Ashley reviews her schedule for the next month to see what meetings she can reschedule. Unfortunately, although Ashley estimates the line shack work will take two weeks, there may be rain delays.

By bedtime, Ashley is tired and falls into bed. Sleep comes quickly, but so does a reoccurring nightmare. She wakes to a soaked bed wishing Jeremy was there to hold her. Finally, at 2:00 am, Ashley is wide awake, changing the sheets on her bed and throwing the sweat-soaked ones into the washer. She enters the kitchen, grabs her comfort food of chips and queso, and turns on the TV.

What is that knocking sound, Ashley wonders, opening her eyes? She looks at the clock on the mantle and sees it's 10:00 am, and the knocking is coming from her door. She yells just a minute and slowly makes her way there. She jerks open the door to find a man with an enormous vase of yellow roses Ashley has ever seen.

"You must have the wrong address," she tells the man.

"No, ma'am. I don't think so. Are you Ashley Winslow?" Ashley nods. "Then these are for you." He hands the vase to Ashley and leaves.

It takes both hands to hold the vase, so Ashley has to close the door with her foot. Next, she sets the vase on the dining table and searches for a card. It takes several seconds because of the number of roses, but Ashley finally locates it. She opens the card and reads, "Ashley, I can be an ass sometimes, and I apologize profusely. I will explain some things next time I see you. In the meantime, you have my number if you need someone to hold you close. I'm staying in Vegas. Jeremy."

Wow! I bet there are four dozen roses here, Ashley thinks, looking at the bouquet. That was very sweet. I wonder how he got my address. From Wesley, of course, her inner voice answers. Ashley picks up her phone, trying to decide what to say in her text to Jeremy. She finally types, "thank you for the beautiful roses. I can be an ass, too. You don't have to explain anything to me. Thank you for the offer to hold me. I could have used it last night." Ashley presses send and then is hit with regret. I shouldn't have told him about last night. Oh well, stuff happens.

After a breakfast of toast made from stale bread, Ashley dresses in shorts, a t-shirt, and sneakers. She pulls her long black hair into a ponytail, grabs her purse, and opens the door to leave. But when she opens the door, there stands Jeremy. His hair is pulled back into a man bun. He has dressed in a t-shirt with the sleeves cut off, shorts to his knees, and ankle-high sneakers. The sight of him takes her breath away.

Jeremy steps over the threshold and closes the door behind him with his foot. He takes a surprised Ashley into his arms and holds her close. "I'm sorry I wasn't here for you last night," Jeremy whispers in her ear. He leans back and brushes her cheek like he always does with his fingertips. Then he tilts her chin up to look into her eyes.

"Ah, Jeremy," Ashley stammers. "Why are you here?"

"I read your message. It felt like you needed a hug today. So, here I am." Tears fill Ashley's eyes at Jeremy's kind gesture. First, one tear rolls down her cheek, and then another. Jeremy lifts Ashley into his arms and carries her to the sofa. He carefully sits down with her in his lap. Jeremy presses her face into his neck as more tears flow from her eyes. He holds her tightly against his body and lets her cry.

Once the tears have stopped, Ashley lifts her head to look at Jeremy. She raises her hand, caressing his bearded face. "Thank you, Jeremy," she whispers.

"Ashley, are your nightmares becoming more frequent?" he asks softly.

"No, they come and go. It's not always the same nightmare."

"Are they things that happened in your past?'

"Yes. One day, I'll be able to put the past behind me, and they will go away. I have a feeling that time is coming soon," Ashley answers.

"I'll help you in any way I can. I hope you know that." Ashley nods. "Now, Ashley, what are your plans for the day?"

"Well, I was about to leave for the food store. That's it."

"The food store can wait. However, I have someone very important to me I want you to meet. So let's dry those tears and go." Jeremy wipes the remaining tears from Ashley's face before softly kissing her cheek and helping her from his lap.

Chapter 15

JEREMY

*W*ell, this is happening sooner than I had planned, but I think Ashley needs a diversion. Hopefully, it will make her laugh, Jeremy thinks once the pair are in the car.

"Where are we going?" Ashley asks.

"It's a surprise," Jeremy replies. "Sit back and enjoy the short ride." He reaches over, pats Ashley's knee, and then turns the radio on. The station is an oldies station. The pair sings along with the songs as Jeremy drives. Ashley has a beautiful voice; Jeremy determines when he stops singing momentarily to listen to her.

Fifteen minutes later, Jeremy pulls into the driveway of a white two-story house in a Vegas suburb. He and Ashley leave the car and walk to the front door. The door swings open, and a little boy runs out, jumping into Jeremy's arms. "Papa!" the boy screams at the top of his lungs.

"Ashley, I want you to meet my son, Devon. Devon, this is my friend, Ashley."

"Lele," the little boy yells and reaches for Ashley.

Ashley takes him into her arms and grips the little boy against her chest. "Hi, Devon. I am so happy to meet you." She kisses the squirming little boy's cheek.

"Hi, Jeremy," a lady says from the doorway. Ashley glances at her, estimating her age to be in the mid-forties. Then a man slightly taller than the lady appears behind her, smiling.

"Michelle, Mark, this is my friend, Ashley," Jeremy says. The couple offers to shake Ashley's hand, but Devon is wiggling around too much. "Come, Devon. Are you ready to go to the park?"

Ashley sets Devon down as he yells, "Park! Park! Park!" Devon runs into the house, laughing.

"Michelle, I know this is unexpected, and I apologize for not calling," Jeremy says. "But I think Ashley needs an afternoon in the park."

"That's fine, Jeremy," Mark answers for Michelle. "I'll get the car seat for you." Mark turns and leaves the threesome standing at the door.

"Michelle, I'll keep Devon overnight again so you and Mark can have a quiet evening."

"Thanks, Jeremy. Sorry, I forgot my manners. Come into the house."

Yelling, park, park, park, Devon runs up to Jeremy with a bag in his hands.

"What do you have in your bag?" Ashley squats down in front of the little boy.

"Trucks," Devon answers proudly.

Mark walks into the foyer. "I put the car seat in for you. You're all set to go."

"Well, what are we waiting for?" Jeremy says, reaching for Devon's hand. Devon ignores Jeremy's hand and reaches for Ashley's, which surprises Jeremy, Mark and Michelle. Ashley takes the small hand in hers, and together she and Devon walk to the car. "That's interesting," Jeremy remarks, looking at Mark and Michelle, who nod in agreement. "Hey, wait for me," Jeremy yells.

Once they arrive at the park, Devon trots to the sand pile and empties his bag of trucks into the dirt. Jeremy and Ashley sit beside him, and all three plays in the sand for several minutes. Then, satisfied that Devon will entertain himself, Jeremy scoots back to sit on a log surrounding the sand pile. He pats the log beside him for Ashley to join him.

"What a surprise, huh?" Jeremy says once Ashley sits down.

"I'll say. Devon's what, about two years old?" she asks.

"He will be. His birthday is on Saturday. Want to come to his party?"

"Okay. I'd like that very much," Ashley answers, surprising Jeremy. "Will I meet his mother there?"

Jeremy pauses for several seconds. Then he clears his throat. "Devon's mother passed away from a blood clot right after his birth. So she never knew she had a son."

"Oh, Jeremy. I'm so very sorry," Ashley says, laying her hand on Jeremy's arm.

He places his hand on top of hers. "Devon's mother and I dated for several months. During that time, she became pregnant. It was a shock to both of us because she was on the pill. Anyway, we planned to get married after Devon was born, but it wasn't meant to be." Jeremy takes a deep breath. "Mark and Michelle are Devon's grandparents. Because my work involves so much traveling, the three of us decided it would be good for Devon to live with them. So I try to see him as much as possible. That's why I am staying in Vegas. I can spend time with him, plus give Mark and Michelle a break."

"You must have loved Devon's mother very much," Ashley says.

"I did love her, but wasn't in love with her. There's a difference, you know. But I loved her enough to want to marry her and raise our son."

"Papa, pee pee," Devon walks up to Jeremey. Jeremy stands up. "No. Lele, take me."

Jeremy looks down at Ashley, who smiles and stands. "Okay, little man. Give me your hand and let's go."

"Uh, Ashley, are you sure?" Jeremy asks.

"We go this, papa," Ashley answers. She takes Devon's hand and leads him to the restroom. A few minutes later, she and the little boy return. Devon has tears in his eyes. "We had a minor accident," Ashley says, looking at Jeremy before squatting before the little boy. "Devon, it's okay. I have accidents like that all the time. You never get old enough not to have that kind of accident. Why don't we gather your trucks and get some clean clothes?" Ashley wipes away the tears running down the boy's cheeks. Then she places a kiss on his forehead. Devon runs to gather his trucks, with Jeremy and Ashley following.

"I have clean clothes at the hotel, and I think Devon is ready for a nap," Jeremy says. "I'll drop you at home first."

"I have a better idea since you're yawning, too. So, let's stay at my place. I'll throw Devon's clothes in the washer while the two of you nap. Then I'll run to the food store and make dinner for us," Ashley tells him.

"Really? Ashley, that would be great. Devon is easy to please as far as food goes. Mac and cheese are his favorite."

"I can do a delicious mac and cheese," Ashley replies.

Jeremy stands as Devon tosses the last truck in his bag. Jeremy smooths Ashley's cheek with his fingertips and leans close. "Thank you," he whispers in her ear.

Chapter 16

JEREMY

Jeremy strips Devon's clothes off, handing them to Ashley. "What if he has an accident?"

"I can always wash the sheets, and there's a waterproof cover on the mattress, so no worries. Now, the two of you lie down. I'll see you after your nap." She leaves the room as Jeremy tosses a sleepy Devon on the bed and lies beside him.

Devon falls asleep immediately, leaving Jeremy on his side, watching the little boy. *Devon took to Ashley, and she to him,* Jeremy thinks. *I thought it would shock her to learn of Devon, but she seems to have taken it all in stride. Ashley is a truly unique woman. I bet she will make a fantastic mother someday. I hope she can find a man that deserves her. Maybe you could be that man,* Jeremy's inner voice says. *I doubt it. She deserves a lot better than me.* Finally, Jeremy closes his eyes and falls asleep.

Two hours later, Jeremy wakes to the smell of bacon cooking. Devon is still asleep, so Jeremy carefully gets off the bed. Devon's freshly laundered clothes lay on a chair next to the bed. Jeremy enters the kitchen, where he finds Ashley at the cooktop.

"Hi, Ashley."

"Well, sleeping beauty is awake," she says, smiling and turning her head to look at Jeremy.

"Yeah, but it wasn't a kiss that woke me. It was a small foot in the gut. I should wake him soon, or he won't sleep tonight," Jeremy states.

"He'll be fine. I'm sure we'll play trucks until he gets sleepy."

"Ashley, I need to ask a huge favor of you. Only G, Hank and Ida know about Devon. I want to keep it that way."

"Okay, Jeremy. I can keep your secret," she replies.

"Don't you want to know why?"

"Nope. It's your business, not mine."

Jeremy walks over to stand beside Ashley. "You are very good with Devon."

"I had a little brother once," she states.

"What happened to him?" Jeremy asks softly, wanting to know but not wanting to pry.

"I don't know. I thought we might eat a little early. I didn't have lunch, and I'm getting hungry. So here," Ashley hands him a plate full of cooked bacon. "Would you crumble this up for me?"

"Okay," Jeremy replies as a very naked little boy runs into the room, giggling. "Well, someone is up. Hey, let's go put your clothes on." Devon runs back to the bedroom with his dad chasing him. Minutes later, Jeremy returns carrying the boy. "I need to help Lele with dinner. Why don't you play with your trucks in the living room?" Devon runs into the living room, and seconds later, little boy talk and laughter are heard in the kitchen.

"Does Devon like bacon?" Ashley asks while Jeremy crumbles it up, and he nods. Next, Ashley mixes the macaroni and cheese. Then she motions for Jeremy to dump the bacon into the bowl. Finally, she combines it all, puts it in a baking dish, and places it in the oven. "That needs to bake for an hour."

"Good. That gives us time to talk," Jeremy replies. He takes her hand and leads her to the small dining table. Jeremy pulls out a chair for her and then sits. "Let's see. Where did I leave off?" Jeremy pauses for a few seconds and tries to remember. "Oh, yes. It broke my heart when Devon's mother died, and I went a little crazy. No, I went very crazy. There was no limit to what I would do except drugs. That was never an option. I went to Mexico first and different places after that. When you take part in the sports activities I do, all types of women flock to you. I took advantage of them and the situation."

Ashley pulls her hand away from Jeremy's, laying it in her lap. "Jeremy, you don't have to explain all this to me. I don't need to know."

"But I want you to," he replies. "I want you to learn to trust me. The only way I know how is to share my life's sordid history with you, to treat you with respect, and honor your privacy." Jeremy pushes the hair covering her face behind her ear and caresses her cheek. "I've made many mistakes in my life, and with Devon. I don't want to make any with you."

"Papa. Lele. Come play with me," Devon yells from the living room.

"But you will if I let you," Ashley whispers, avoiding Jeremy's caress. "We're coming, Devon." Then, finally, she stands and walks off.

After playing, having dinner, and playing more, Jeremy decides to take Devon to the hotel for the night.

"Ashley, are you still interested in Devon's party on Saturday?" Jeremy asks when he and Devon reach the door to leave.

"Yes, please."

"Okay, the party is at 3:00 pm. I'll pick you up at 2:30." Ashley nods. Jeremy touches her cheek. "Remember, I'm only a phone call or text away if you need me."

"I will. Good night, Jeremy." She opens the door, leans over, and kisses Devon on the cheek. "I'll see you Saturday." The little boy surprises Ashley and Jeremy by wrapping his arms around Ashley's neck and hugging her, bringing tears to her eyes. Jeremy softly kisses away the single tear trickling down Ashley's cheek as she stands.

Chapter 17

ASHLEY

Ashley's meeting with Wesley on Monday morning goes well. She tells him everything, including her talk with G about the house for Jeremy. During the meeting, Wesley tells her he plans to hire a new architect to help with her current projects to free up her time. He has already interviewed three prospective applicants and plans to make an offer on Wednesday this week. Wesley also tells Ashley he's had a few inquiries from Wyoming about her work. He adds he is considering opening up an office there if more interest is generated. The rest of the first week back in the office is filled with Ashley catching up on client meetings. Wesley made an offer to an applicant, which was accepted.

At 2:30 pm on Saturday, there is a tiny knock on Ashley's door. "Hi, Lele!" Devon yells when she opens the door.

"Hi, sweetheart." Ashley leans down and hugs the little boy.

"Hug papa, too," Devon says. Jeremy blushes when Ashley looks up at him. She grins and gives Jeremy a slight hug.

"Are you ready to party?" Jeremy murmurs in her ear. Ashley nods as she grabs her purse and gift for Devon.

"What?" Devon asks as he points at the gift.

"You'll see later, I promise," Ashley replies. Jeremy takes the gift from Ashley as Devon reaches for her hand.

The party is a surprise for Devon. That's why he was with Jeremy and not at home. The little boy squeals with delight when he, his papa, and Lele walk into the home's backyard. Cake, ice cream and punch were abundant for the children. There was an assortment of liquor and wine for the adults. Mike and Michelle had invited a small group of neighbors and families from Devon's Mother's Day Out program.

After a while, Devon opened his gifts. Many were trucks for toddlers. Jeremy's gift was a personalized wooden semi-truck, but Ashley's gift caused a little confusion for Devon. Her gift was a toddler tool set. She explained he will need it when he goes to see G, which made him happy.

At 6:00, the party began winding down. Tired parents loaded their children up and headed home. As they leave a happy but tired Devon, Jeremy promises to see him the next day. Ashley hugs him and says she will see him soon.

Once in the car, Jeremy says, "what's with the toolset?"

"Did you really think I could work on the line shack alone? I need help, Jeremy, and I can't think of a better helper," Ashley replies with a grin.

"I don't expect you to babysit, Ashley."

"I know, but I enjoy being around Devon. He makes me happy."

"What about his papa? Does he make you happy?" Jeremy asks shyly.

Ashley blushes at the question. "Yes, his papa makes me happy, too."

Jeremy reaches for her hand. "Will you have dinner with me, or are you too full of cake and ice cream?"

"Are you asking me on a date?"

"Not tonight," Jeremy answers. "But I promise, I will soon. Tonight is just dinner between a man and woman talking business. I want to hear about your plans for the line shack."

"Okay. Can we eat something light, though? I don't have much room for anything else," Ashley replies, smiling at Jeremy.

The new hire starts work on Monday of Ashley's second week back in the office. She shadows Ashley and attends meetings with her. Ashley is pleased with the woman's knowledge and feels good about leaving her workload in the woman's hands. On Wednesday night, Ashley texts Jeremy she can leave on Saturday, and everything was in place for her to be gone for approximately one month.

By Friday morning, Ashley hasn't had a reply from Jeremy and gets concerned. She texts him to ask if everything is okay. He replies that he's just been busy. He says he'll pick her up at 9:00 am Saturday so she won't have to leave her car at the airport.

9:00 am Saturday comes around, and no Jeremy. Ashley is packed and ready to go, but refuses to text him. Finally, he shows up at 10:00. Jeremy looks tired, and his clothes are wrinkled. He smells of perfume and bourbon. It upsets Ashley greatly, but she doesn't say anything about it. She just hands him a suitcase and closes the door behind her. When Jeremy offers to take Ashley's second suitcase from her hand, she says she can manage.

The drive to Devon's house is silent, with Ashley staring out her window the entire way. When they reach Devon's home, Jeremy leaves Ashley sitting in the car while he gets the little boy and his suitcase. Jeremy has to make a second trip to retrieve a bag of toys and the toolset Ashley gave Devon. The little boy chatters all the way to the airport. Ashley talks to Devon while Jeremy gives one-word answers to Devon's questions or grunts.

Bill, the co-pilot, loads everyone's luggage onto the plane. Jeremy quickly showers in the jet's lavatory, then goes to the cockpit, leaving Ashley to care for Devon. She buckles the child into a seat next to her. Ashley looks up at the plane's cockpit and notices Jeremy watching her. She ignores him and focuses on entertaining Devon. Finally, the door closes, and the plane takes off.

The flight is uneventful, and Devon is easily entertained with a movie, giving Ashley time to reflect on the morning. Obviously, Jeremy had been with a woman, and that was why he was late picking me up. Jeremy is a grown man, she thinks. I don't care what he does in his free time, but I hate Devon saw him like that. You're jealous, her inner voice says. No, I'm not, Ashley answers in her mind. I'm disappointed, but not jealous. If you say so, the inner voice replies. Devon didn't seem to notice his dad's actions or appearance. Maybe he's used to it. I hope not. That doesn't set a good example for Devon, Ashley determines.

When the plane finally lands, G is at the airport waiting. Devon runs to greet her, with Ashley following. Jeremy and Bill load the luggage into Jeremy's SUV. After hugging Devon and getting settled in the car seat, G looks at Ashley with a raised eyebrow, sensing the tension between Ashley and Jeremy. Ashley shrugs her shoulders and climbs into the front passenger seat while G sits in the back with Devon.

A little boy's conversation with his great-grandmother is the only sound in the SUV for the drive to the ranch. Jeremy grunts a few times when G asks him questions. Ashley never says a word. When they reach the ranch, Ashley asks Hank for the keys to the four-wheeler, insisting she will stay in the line shack while overseeing the work. G protests, but Jeremy never says a word. In fact, he ignores the entire conversation. Hank helps Ashley load her luggage, and then she heads to her home, away from home, for the next four weeks.

Even though there's no closet space in the line shack, Ashley unpacks and puts her things away as best she can. Next, she looks over the food selection, attempting to find something for lunch. Then, there's a knock on the door, and G sticks her head in.

"I brought you some lunch," G says, setting a plate on the tiny table. "What's going on between you and Jeremy?"

"Straight to the point, aren't you, G?" Ashley asks with a laugh. G nods. "Nothing is going." G cocks her head, and one corner of her mouth turns upwards. "Okay, first, he was late getting me. Then, when he shows up, he looks like he slept in his clothes and smells of perfume and bourbon. I didn't think that was an appropriate way for Devon to see his dad."

"Well, I agree with you on that. Did you say anything to Jeremy about it?"

"No, I haven't spoken to Jeremy since Devon's birthday party a week ago," Ashley answers.

"Is that why you want to stay here, so that you can avoid him?"

"No, I want to stay here because the supplies will be delivered beginning Tuesday, and there's some preliminary work I need to do. Were you able to find some workers?" Ashley asks.

"Yes, I found three. They will be here early Tuesday morning. Are you sure you want to stay here? It's very rustic."

"I know, and yes."

"Okay. Well, just know that Devon is in Jeremy's room. Your room is available. At least join us for meals. Don't isolate yourself from the rest of us because of Jeremy's childish actions," G says as she turns and leaves.

Ashley sits and goes over her plans while she eats the lunch G brought. I need to go into town tomorrow. I'll see if I can borrow a pickup. After eating, Ashley walks down to her favorite place on the mountainside and gazes at the valley below. Then she lies down on the fresh grass and watches the clouds float across the sky as she did as a child. Ashley hears Devon's laughter from the house and smiles, thinking about the little brother she had. After a while, she drifts off to sleep.

"Miss Ashley, wake up," a soft voice whispers in Ashley's ear. She opens her eyes to find Tyler bending over her.

"Oh, I guess I fell asleep," Ashley says, sitting up quickly.

Tyler grins at her. "I hate to wake you, but the sun is going down. You'll get chilled out here."

"Ah, thanks, Tyler."

"I understand you will do some work on the cabin. Are you planning to live in the cabin?"

"Why, yes, I am. For a while, anyway," Ashley answers. "Why?"

"I need to show you something important." Tyler offers his hand to Ashley, and she accepts it before rising to her feet. She follows him to the cabin and inside. He goes to a drawer near the fireplace and opens it.

"This is a two-way radio. We use it out here because the cell phone service is sketchy." Tyler shows it to Ashley and shows her how it works and who it contacts. "If you have any problem or something frightens you, just call someone on it. One of the other cowboys or I can be here in a few minutes. It will take Hank a little longer. Now, let me show you how to start the generator, and then I'll bring in more firewood for you. Can you think of anything else you might need?"

"Not at the moment, Tyler. Thanks for doing this for me. I guess everyone assumed I knew these things."

"Everyone seems busy with the little boy. I think it surprised them you wanted to stay here."

"Ah, Tyler, can I borrow a pickup on the ranch tomorrow? I need to go into town and buy a few things?"

"I'm free tomorrow. I'll take you. What time would you like to go?" Tyler asks.

"About 10:00. I think the stores I need to go to will be open by then," Ashley replies.

"Okay. Meet me at the house at 10:00. Now, let's see about the generator."

Chapter 18

JEREMY

Jeremy deliberately kept Devon from taking an afternoon nap in hopes the little boy would go to sleep early and sleep all night long. It works, so Jeremy takes Ashley, his dad's credit card. Unfortunately, he was so hungover this morning that he forgot to give it to her.

He walks toward the line shack and hears laughter. Although dark, he hides behind some trees and sees Tyler and Ashley sitting on the porch, talking. He sees Ashley rear her head back, laughing. Her long black hair flows across her back. She never laughs like that with me. You idiot, his inner voice says. You've never made her laugh like that. Have you ever made her laugh at all? Shut up, Jeremy tells the voice. Why do I care about Tyler even being here? Because you're jealous. It could be you on that porch if you would think with your head instead of below your waist.

Disgusted with himself, Jeremy heads back to the house. I'll come back after Tyler leaves. But when he returns two hours later, the line shack is dark and quiet. I guess Ashley went to bed. I have a key. I could go in and wake her, probably making her more upset with me. Instead, Jeremy takes the envelope with the credit card and hangs it on a nail on the front door. There, he says to himself, she will find it easily.

"Is this the same bad mood or a new one?" G asks as Jeremy and Devon walk into the dining room for breakfast.

"What?" Jeremy says, helping Devon into his high chair.

"You've been in a horrible mood ever since you arrived? I just wanted to know if it was the same or a new mood."

"It is a continuation with additional anger," Jeremy replies snidely.

"I suppose the additional part has to do with Tyler driving Ashley into town this morning," G says, watching Jeremy closely.

"And being at the cabin last night when I went to take her a credit card." Too ashamed to look at G, Jeremy fills a plate of food for Devon.

"Want to see Lele," Devon pipes up, fueling the fire.

"Your papa will take you there after Ashley returns," G says. "He needs to talk to Ashley later, anyway."

Jeremy looks at his grandmother, surprised. "I do?" G just gives him a look that says Jeremy is stupid.

Mid-afternoon, Jeremy hears Tyler's big pickup pass by the house. He waits thirty minutes. "Devon, let's go see Lele." He takes the small boy's hand, and they walk to the line shack. Jeremy sees Tyler helping Ashley unload the back of the pickup and starts to leave.

Devon jerks his hand away and runs toward Ashley. "Lele! Lele!"

"Hi, little man," Ashley says, dropping a bag on the ground so she can catch the little boy. "What a delightful surprise. I've missed you," she tells him, kissing him on the cheek.

"Miss you too," Devon replies with a big grin.

"Ah, Devon and I came to see if we could help," Jeremy says.

"I'm afraid you're too late," Tyler says, glaring at Jeremy. "Ashley and I just finished up. Tyler leans against the back of the pickup and smirks.

"I help," Devon yells.

"Great, Devon. I'll let you help me carry this bag into the house," Ashley says, feeling the tension building between the two men. She and Devon pick up the bag and carry it inside the house. Seconds later, Devon emerges from the cabin with a red lollipop. Ashley follows behind.

"Thanks for your help, Tyler," she says. Then, sensing he is being dismissed, Tyler nods, gets in his pickup, and drives off. "Devon, why don't you sit on this rock and have your lollipop? You shouldn't walk or run with it in your mouth."

Devon nods and sits down. Ashley walks to the far end of the porch and picks up a bag she left sitting there. When she turns around, Jeremy stands so close behind her she bumps into him. "Thanks for the credit card. I used it to buy supplies," she waves her arm at two piles of items she bought.

"I'm sorry I made you mad," Jeremy says, brushing her cheek. Ashley jerks her head away and steps backward. "I can be a real jerk sometimes."

"I'm not angry, Jeremy. Just disappointed. You don't have to apologize to me. What you do in your life is no concern of mine. If you feel the need to apologize to someone, apologize to Devon," Ashley says, looking directly into Jeremy's eyes. He hears her words but sees the pain in her eyes.

"You're right, but in my defense, I'm still learning this father stuff. Right now, though, your feelings are most important to me."

Ashley drops the bag and puts her hands on her hips. "What exactly do you want from me, Jeremy? It's almost like you're two different people. One person is kind and gentle. He holds me when I cry. The other person is cold and uncaring. I feel like I'm being punished for God knows what. Please leave. Devon can stay, and I'll take him back to the house later. But I want you to go."

"Let's go, Devon," Jeremy says, turning his back on Ashley. "Lele is busy. Maybe you can come back tomorrow." He scoops up the little boy and walks off.

"Papa, don't cry," Devon says when Jeremy picks him up.

"Be quiet, Devon," Jeremy says, hoping Ashley didn't hear the comment.

Chapter 19

ASHLEY

Did I hear Devon right? Ashley wonders as she watches Jeremy carry Devon to the house? Surely not. I'm not sure Jeremy has it inside himself to feel emotions of remorse. Maybe he did when Devon's mother was alive, but not now. Oh well, not my problem; Ashley shrugs and begins sorting the supplies she bought. She has much to do tomorrow before the trucks and workers arrive on Tuesday.

After a couple of hours of work, Ashley realizes she's hungry. She knows Hank has dinner ready at the house, but she doesn't want to be around Jeremy. Ashley goes inside and eats a protein bar she bought this morning while she and Tyler were in town. She grabs a bottle of water and walks down the mountainside to watch the sky change colors as the sun sets behind her.

It is almost dark when Ashley senses something behind her. She turns her head slightly and sees a movement from the corner of her eye. "How long have you been sitting there watching me?" Ashley asks.

"For a while," Jeremy replies. "Can I join you? I want to talk to you."

"No, just stay where you are. Maybe we can work out a truce or something if we don't look at each other. I'm going to be here for four weeks. I can't continue to take one step forward with you and two back."

"What do you mean?" Jeremy asks.

"I know you share things with me and do things to prove that you trust me. Then you won't talk to me or just flat-out ignore me. Jeremy, I want to learn to trust you. I really do, but you make it hard for me when you're like that," Ashley says, pulling her knees up and leaning back on her hands. "I know you get frustrated with me. I do myself. But the hurt, pain, and shame caused by someone I trusted have left me vulnerable. I'm tired of feeling what I do, but I believe that whoever I trust will, at some time or another, cause me to have those feelings again." Ashley pauses. "Jeremy, can I ask you two questions?" She senses he moves a little closer.

"You can ask me anything, Ashley, and I'll answer honestly."

"Okay. Jeremy, you know yourself better than anyone. First, can I trust you with my secrets, and second, can we be friends?" She feels him scoot closer.

"Sometimes, I don't know myself at all. I think I do. Then I do something stupid, and it hurts someone. Lately, that someone is you. The last two years have been difficult. I feel as though my heart tells me one thing, my brain another, and I do something another part of me tells me to do. I believe deeply that you can trust me with your secrets. I won't judge you, that I promise. But I want desperately to be friends with you. You are so different from any woman I have ever known. I have Devon to consider now, and you are so gentle and patient with him. That's very important to me. Perhaps, by being friends, you can help me find who Jeremy Marsh really is and to be the man Devon needs me to be."

"Jeremy, please come lie beside me," Ashley says. "Let's look at the stars, and maybe, just maybe, we can begin healing each other." She lies on her back. Jeremy crawls to her. He lies on his back beside Ashley but doesn't touch her. She reaches for his hand, clasps it, and they watch the stars move across the sky.

When the moon peeks over the mountains, Jeremy asks, "did you bring a flashlight?"

"No. I did not know I would be here this long," Ashley replies.

Wolves howl in the valley. "I better get you to the line shack. The wolves are moving in this direction." Jeremy stands and helps Ashley up. He walks her to the cabin door. "Can you see well enough to get around?" Ashley nods. "I wish you would move back to your bedroom so I can hear you if you have a nightmare."

"I need to do this, Jeremy," Ashley replies.

"Okay, good night, my friend," Jeremy says as he caresses her cheek. He opens the door for Ashley and then leaves.

Shortly after falling asleep, one of Ashley's nightmares invades her subconscious. She is sleeping with her little brother beside her. Her arm lies across his stomach to ensure he doesn't fall off the bed. Still, in the nightmare, Ashley suddenly wakes up, and her little brother is gone. "The baby! The baby," she yells. Then, a faceless man appears in the doorway. "The baby is gone," Ashley yells again. "I know," the man says. "Now shut up and go back to sleep."

Ashley wakes sweating profusely. Her gown and bedclothes covering her are soaked. Then the wet top sheet and blanket lift, and strong, muscular arms wrap around Ashley, pulling her close.

"How did you know?" she whispers.

"Somehow, I could sense that you needed me," Jeremy whispers in her ear.

"Everything is wet," Ashley cries.

"Shhh. I know. We'll worry about that later."

Chapter 20

JEREMY

Ashley is right. Everything is wet, including her, Jeremy thinks as he guides her head to his shoulder. At least Ashley went back to sleep quickly. That was really strange. I was sound asleep for one minute, and then I felt Ashley needing me. I wish I had gotten here sooner. Maybe the nightmare wouldn't have been so bad.

Jeremy feels the wetness of Ashley's gown and bedclothes seep into his pajama pants. There's no way I can sleep like this, but he determines he's not getting up until Ashley's fully relaxed. Jeremy holds her, recalling their earlier conversation. Ashley wants to trust him, so he needs to get his life straight to prove he can be trusted. I told her the truth. I'm lost at least half the time. I haven't found my place in life. I thought Devon would help ground me, but a little boy can do only so much. G would say I need to grow up.

Ashley turns on her side, facing away from Jeremy. She relaxed and breathed softly. He climbs out of bed, eases out the door, and returns to his bedroom. He checks on Devon and then climbs into bed.

"Papa. Wake up," Devon calls from his bed. Jeremy turns and looks at his mini-me.

"If you had a beard, you'd look just like me," Jeremy tells him. "Let's shower and get some breakfast. We need to go see if we can help Lele this morning."

Devon laughs as his papa picks him up. "Yea! Lele! Me love Lele!"

"I know you do, little man, and I can tell she loves you, too." Jeremy squeezes Devon and tickles him.

It surprises Jeremy to see Ashley sitting at the dining room table when he and Devon enter. Devon runs to her and jumps into her lap, almost knocking them over onto the floor. He throws his tiny arms around Ashley's neck and surprises everyone by saying, "me love, Lele."

"I love you, too, Devon," Ashley replies, hugging me tightly.

"Papa love Lele. Lele love papa."

Jeremy's jaw drops, and he sees Ashley blush. He looks at G and notices a massive grin on her face. The little boy jumps off her lap and reaches for Jeremy to place him in his high chair.

"Well, now that's been settled, I think we can eat," G announces.

"Ashley, Devon and I wondered if we could help you today," Jeremy says when everyone finishes eating.

"Tools!" Devon yells, causing everyone to laugh.

"I would love to have help today, especially yours, Devon. I have some dirt that needs to be moved, so you better get two or three trucks too," Ashley replies.

"Papa, down," Devon says, holding up his little arms. Jeremy takes him from the chair and sets him on the floor. Immediately, little legs run into the living area and quickly return with a bag of toys. "Ready," Devon announces.

Jeremy carries the bag of toys as Ashley walks beside him, and Devon runs ahead to the line shack.

"Are you okay?" Jeremy asks in a low voice.

"I am. Jeremy, thank you for last night. But I don't understand how you knew," Ashley replies.

"I can't answer it. I was sound asleep. Suddenly, I woke up and said, Ashley. I got up and ran down here as fast as I could."

"I'm sorry about the wet bed. I should have gotten up and changed it."

Jeremy grabs her arm and turns Ashley, so she is facing him. "Ashley," he says, caressing her cheek. "No, baby girl. You needed to be held much more than up changing sheets." Ashley leans into the caress and closes her eyes.

"That feels good," she states, then backs away and returns to following Devon.

Jeremy stands there momentarily, watching Ashley. I believe I woke up in the twilight zone this morning, Jeremy says to himself. First, Devon announced Ashley and I love each other. Then I call her baby girl. Next, she leaned into the caress and said it felt good. Jeremy looks up at the sky. "What is going on?" he murmurs to the heavens.

Ashley assigns Devon to move a small pile of dirt six inches to another. Jeremy helps Ashley as much as possible, but mainly stands behind her, claiming he needs to hold the ladder as she climbs. He takes the opportunity to appreciate her jeans' snug fit across her butt.

At lunchtime, Jeremy takes Devon to the house, feeds the little boy, and puts him down for a nap. He asks G to watch over the little boy so he can return and help Ashley and take her lunch. The pair work until dinnertime. G kept Devon at the house all afternoon, so Jeremy packs up the toys. Then he and Ashley go to the house for dinner. After dinner, Ashley returns to the line shack alone while Jeremy plays with Devon and his trucks.

Chapter 21

ASHLEY

The smell of coffee wakes Ashley. She turns over and opens her eyes to find Jeremy standing by the small propane stove, smiling at her.

"Good morning, my favorite architect," he says with a wink.

"What are you doing here so early?" Ashley asks, climbing out of bed.

"Well, the truthful answer is, I figured you wanted to get an early start. But the man in me says it's for the view."

Ashley looks down at her thin, almost see-thru oversized t-shirt. Blushing, she quickly grabs a blanket off the bed to cover herself. "I, ah, I haven't had time to do laundry. I found this in one chest."

"I think it was an excellent choice. I will take my coffee to the porch and let you dress. I brought breakfast for us." Ashley smiles as Jeremy turns around and leaves.

"What can I do today?" Jeremy asks.

"You can direct traffic," Ashley replies. Jeremy looks at her, confused. "You can show the workers where to park first. Then wait down at the main road for the trucks. I need the truck hauling the cistern here, and then the others can follow. Since the trail is so narrow, they must come one at a time, unload, and then back out."

"Okay, I can do that. I'm getting excited. I can't wait to see the finished cabin. I imagine the workers will be here shortly, so I'll go now." Jeremy caresses her cheek with his fingertips and smiles as he leaves.

"Thank you, Jeremy, for everything."

"See you later, baby girl."

"Baby girl," Ashley softly says as she watches Jeremy walk away. Man, he looks so hot today. Jeremy's wearing his usual black boots, green spandex shorts to his knees, and a white muscle shirt. The tight shorts tighten across Jeremy's thigh muscles as he walks. The muscle shirt shows off his broad shoulders. His dark brown wavy hair is tied up in a man bun. I've seen men dressed similarly, but none ever affected me the way he does, Ashley thinks. She shakes her head to clear her thoughts.

The day is busy and ends as the sun sets. Jeremy does a great job with the trucks. The three new men are seasoned construction workers, and all the supplies arrived intact. Devon helps his papa with the trucks and even rides to the line shack in one truck. Hank fixes a massive lunch for everyone, but most importantly, the weather is perfect.

After dinner, Ashley sits in her favorite spot overlooking the valley. She's tired but excited to get started the following day. Ashey feels Jeremy approach before he sits down next to her.

He brushes her hair back as he sits down. "Tired, baby girl?" Jeremy asks.

"Yes, very much. I'll probably be sore tomorrow."

"Come back to the house with me and take a long, hot bath. I bet G has some bath salts lying around."

"That sounds like a wonderful idea. I'll grab some clothes and be right back," Ashley tells him.

"Ida said to bring your laundry with you. So she can do it for you tomorrow."

"She doesn't have to. I can do it tomorrow night," Ashley replies.

"I told her you would say that, but she insisted." Ashley nods and goes to the cabin.

When she returns, Jeremy stands and takes a basket of clothes from her. "Ashley, would you go out with me this Saturday night he asks?"

"What do you have in mind, Mr. Marsh?"

"I was thinking of dinner and dancing. How does that sound to you?"

"Jeremy, I never learned how to dance," Ashley answers, looking down at her feet. "I didn't bring anything to wear to something like that."

"Please, just say yes and trust me, Ashley. It's important to me," Jeremy tells her.

"Okay. I would love to go out with you. Is this a date?" she looks at him and shyly asks.

"You better believe it is," Jeremy answers, taking her hand. "Let's go get you that bath."

The following morning, Ashley and the workers are hard at work while Jeremy helps Devon work on his dirt pile several hundred feet away from the cabin. The two-way radio is lying on the porch and crackles.

"Jeremy, get to the house now," G's panicked voice says. "Jarod just drove up."

"Crap," Jeremy says, rising to his feet. "Devon, stay here and don't move until Ashley tells you that you can. Okay?"

"K, papa." Jeremy trots up to the house while Ashley watches.

Thirty minutes later, Jeremy, Jarod, and G walk toward the line shack. Ashley sees them coming and climbs down the ladder.

"Hello, Ms. Winslow. My father saw the supplies purchase and sent me to see how things are progressing."

"Things are going well, Mr. Marsh," Ashley replies.

"Why are you working on the line shack?"

"Well, much of the information about the land isn't available since it is private property and has been in the family for generations. So, I have to improvise."

Jarod spies Devon. "Whose brat is that?"

Ashley looks Jarod right in the eyes and replies, "that is my son, Devon."

"What's he doing here?" Jarod asks.

"I could not find a sitter for him for the four weeks I'm here. I can assure you he is not interfering with my work," Ashley says, her face red in anger. "But, Mr. Marsh, if you disapprove of him being here, please report it to your father; he can fire me if he likes. I have clients in Vegas that I could be tending to instead of being here."

"Ms. Winslow, regardless of any reservations I may have, I doubt my father will fire you. Good day." Jarod turns and walks back to the house. G smiles at Ashley and gives her a thumbs-up before following Jarod.

Jeremy walks over to Ashley, taking her hand in his. "Ashley, you didn't have to do that."

"Yes, Jeremy, I did. I promised to keep your secret. Besides, he shouldn't have called Devon a brat. It made me mad," Ashley says, smiling.

Jeremy leans over and whispers, "I'll return as soon as possible. Thank you, baby girl."

Chapter 22

ASHLEY

"Dammit, Hank. You should have seen the expression on Jarod's face when Ashley told him off," Jeremy says.

"Dam it, dam it, dam it," Devon shouts. G looks over at Jeremy and shakes her head, smiling as she does. Hank stands behind her, snickering.

"Devon, that's not a nice word, and I shouldn't have said it. So let's not repeat it anymore, okay, big guy?" Jeremy says. Devon nods, stuffing more mac and cheese into his mouth.

"Like father, like son," Ashley remarks, and everyone bursts out laughing except Jeremy. He tries to look like his feelings are hurt but fails miserably and laughs as well.

After dinner, Ashley takes a hot bath. Then Jeremy walks her to the cabin. "I know you're tired, so sleep well, Ashley," Jeremy says, then turns and leaves her on the porch yawning.

She walks into the cabin and sees several packages and a box lying on the bed. First, she opens the box. Inside is a pair of costly four-inch red heels with red soles. Next, she opens each package carefully. A red sleeveless dress with a sweetheart neckline is in the first package. The following package includes the most beautiful lingerie she has ever seen. The third package holds a red shawl that matches the dress. Ashley spies a smaller box inside the shawl's bag. She opens the box and finds a ruby necklace with matching earrings.

Ashley quickly strips her clothes off and tries the clothing on. Everything fits perfectly, especially the lingerie. "Wow! Either Jeremy went through my clothes looking for sizes, or he's a talented guesser. I wish I had a full-length mirror," Ashley says aloud.

"Ashley," G's voice says from the porch. "Do you need a mirror, my dear?"

Jerking the door open, Ashley looks at the petite woman standing on the porch with a full-length mirror in her hands. "Oh, G. You're a lifesaver. Come in."

"You look beautiful," G says, looking at Ashley from head to toe.

"Thanks. You did an excellent job."

"Ashley, I didn't do anything but bring the mirror. Jeremy did all of that on his own. I have to say my grandson has great taste."

"Did he pick out the lingerie too?" Ashley asks.

"I guess, but then I always told him if he was going to do something, do it all the way or don't do it at all. So now, why don't you come to the house Saturday afternoon and we'll do your hair and makeup? He won't recognize you when we finish," G says with a huge grin.

"Sounds great. Did he tell you I have never danced?"

"He did. He also said he asked you to trust him. So you'll be in excellent hands, Ashley. Don't worry."

The rest of the week goes by fast for Ashley. Between her and the workers, the job is on schedule. Friday evening, Jeremy tells Ashley he plans to take Devon to the park Saturday afternoon so she can do whatever she needs in her bedroom and the communal bathroom. After Jeremy and Devon leave, Ashley loads up her new clothes and goes to the house.

Chapter 23

JEREMY

Ashley's bedroom door is closed when Jeremy returns home. He showers and dresses in a light blue button-down shirt, navy slacks and black loafers. Surprised at his nervousness, he checks himself in the mirror several times before leaving for the living room.

Jeremy paces the floor while G, Hank, Ida and Devon watch. A few minutes later, Ashley enters the room when Jeremy's back is turned. She stands there quietly, smiling, waiting for him to turn around.

Finally, he turns around, and the sight takes his breath away. He looks at Ashley from the top of her head to the red shoes on her feet. Her long jet-black hair is arranged so her ears and slender neck are visible with the ruby necklace and earrings. The sweetheart neckline of the red dress is low enough to show a hint of cleavage. The dress hugs her curvy body perfectly and hits her mid-thigh, revealing her legs. The red heels accentuate her dainty ankles.

"Ashley, you look like a goddess," Jeremy says.

"Thank you, and you look very handsome Jeremy," she blushes.

"Kiss, kiss, kiss," Devon yells from the floor, surrounded by his trucks.

"Okay, son," Jeremy says as he strides over to Ashley and kisses her softly on the cheek. "Shall we go before Devon says anything else?" Jeremy breathes in her ear. Ashley giggles and nods.

Jeremy and Ashley go to his favorite Italian restaurant for a quiet dinner. The pair laugh and talk, enjoying each other's company. Afterward, Jeremy takes her to his favorite bar with a small dance floor. The music is fast and loud as they enter the bar and find a table. Jeremy can tell by Ashley's body language she's nervous.

After they sit down, several women stop by the table, flirting with Jeremy and asking him to dance. The women totally ignore Ashley, even though Jeremy tries to introduce her. Ashley urges Jeremy to dance with the women.

"Ashley, you are my date tonight. We are a couple and will stay that way."

Finally, the DJ announces it's her break time, and there will be nonstop slow music until she returns.

"Come, it's time for you to dance with me," Jeremy says, holding his hand to Ashley as he stands. She accepts his hand, and he leads her to the dance floor. He lifts her chin to force her to look into his eyes. "Now, think about the times I've held you in my lap. Put your arms around my neck and lay your head on my shoulder." Ashley does as instructed. "Close your eyes and listen to the music. Let it flow through you. Your body is against mine and will follow my movements. I promise."

"Okay, Ashley whispers in Jeremy's ear. The music begins, and Jeremy feels Ashley relax against him. Her warm breath touches his chest. He begins to dance slowly, guiding Ashley around the dance floor.

The couple dances to three songs before Ashley lifts her head, looks into Jeremy's eyes, and smiles. Next, he lowers his head, touching his nose to hers, his dark brown eyes gazing into her bright blue eyes.

At the end of the fourth song, Jeremy can no longer resist. He softly kisses Ashley's perfect cupid bow lips. She looks at him in surprise and rests her head on his shoulder.

After one more song, Jeremy looks down at Ashley and whispers, "kiss me, Ashley."

She looks up at him. Expecting her to kiss him, Jeremy is stunned when Ashley says, "I can't."

"You can't, or you won't?"

"I can't, Jeremy," Ashley answers.

Jeremy suddenly releases her and takes a step back. "We're leaving," he tells her harshly and walks away. He makes it to the SUV first and gets inside. Ashley finally gets in, carrying her heels in one hand. Jeremy starts the SUV and drives off. He says nothing to Ashley on the forty-five-minute drive home.

When he pulls into the driveway and turns the ignition off, Ashley says, "Jeremy, please let me explain."

"I don't want to talk about it," he states and limbs out of the SUV, leaving Ashley to exit the vehicle and walk to the line shack alone.

Chapter 24

ASHLEY

Ashley cries all the way to the line shack. The full moon provides light inside the cabin, so Ashley strips off all the clothing and shoes, throwing them into a heap on the floor. Finally, she climbs into bed and cries herself to sleep.

Early the following day, Ashley is up, letting her hair down and washing the streaked makeup off her face. She eyes the pile of clothing on the floor and kicks it before dressing in her usual work attire. Ashley decides not to eat anything because her stomach is tied in knots.

Ashley is bent over working on something between the cabin and the cistern when she hears someone walk up.

"Ashley, I want to talk about last night," Jeremy says harshly.

"Well, I don't. You had your chance last night," she replies in a strained voice.

"I've had time to calm down a little. I want to discuss why you said you couldn't kiss me."

Ashley takes a deep breath, stands upright, and turns to face Jeremy. She removes her gloves slowly, one at a time, glaring at Jeremy. Next, she removes her cap, placing the gloves inside the hat. "Fine. You want to talk? We'll talk," she yells. "Do you want to have this conversation out here or in the cabin?"

"I don't care," Jeremy yells back. "I want to know why you wouldn't kiss me when I asked you to?"

Even though Ashley glares at Jeremy in anger, her eyes fill with shame. "I wanted to kiss you, Jeremy. I wanted to so much, but I couldn't because I don't know how," Ashley whispers. "I'm twenty-six years old, and I've never kissed a man. You are the first man ever to kiss me. I'm sorry I disappointed you." Ashley throws her cap and gloves at Jeremy and walks off, hanging her head. She walks around the cabin and down into the valley, sits on a large boulder with her elbows on her knees, and sobs.

Chapter 25

JEREMY

Jeremy drops to his knees, feeling like he just took a punch in the heart. Not only did he back Ashley into a corner, forcing an answer, but he also embarrassed her. He looks to the heavens and says, "God, we both know I'm not a praying man, but I need your help to make this right between Ashley and me." He kneels there for several minutes, trying to figure out what to do. Finally, he slowly gets up and makes his way down to Ashley.

He kneels in front of Ashley, tears rolling down his face. "Ashley, I'm so sorry."

"Jeremy, please leave me alone," Ashley whispers.

"Not this time, baby girl. We will talk like adults for once and, hopefully, work this out." Jeremy wipes his tears away and then hers. "Come with me. I want to show you something." Ashley shakes her head, still refusing to look at him. "Please, Ashley, come with me." She nods and stands.

Jeremy stands and takes her hand. He leads her farther into the valley and stops near a barely trickling stream, releasing her hand. "See this stream?" he points to the ground. "It is fed by an underground spring. You are like this underground spring. The water is clean and refreshing. But like this spring, you provide information about yourself in a trickle."

Ashley watches the water move up from the ground into the small stream. "So?"

"So, I am the rancher. I watch the water slowly move up into the stream and wonder if the spring will provide enough water for the cattle. So I make assumptions while I watch it. I assume if there isn't enough water, I will have to make other arrangements for the cattle because I don't know how much water is underground in the spring." Jeremy pauses. "That's what I did with you. I made assumptions based on my lack of knowledge about you. I assumed you didn't want to kiss me because you had a husband or boyfriend or were coming off a bad breakup. I assumed you didn't like me or something about me that made you not want to kiss me."

Ashley finally looks up at Jeremy. "Based upon my incorrect assumptions, I forced you to give me an answer. You gave me information you may or may not have given me later. In doing so, I embarrassed and hurt you, and it breaks my heart that I did. All I can do now is ask for your forgiveness and hope with every fiber of my being that you will."

Ashley and Jeremy stand silently, searching each other's eyes for several minutes. Ashley's eyes search for trust and understanding. Jeremy's eyes search hers for forgiveness and a chance at a relationship.

Finally, Ashley speaks. "Jeremy, I forgive you. I would have told you, eventually. I didn't think it would happen this soon. We are still working on our friendship. To me, kissing a man involves more than friendship. Does that make sense?"

"It does. Perhaps I want more with you than just friendship." Jeremy caresses Ashley's cheek. "But you have to want it, too, or a relationship of that type won't work."

Ashley smiles and covers the hand on her cheek with her own. "I think I want more than friendship, too, Jeremy, but I need you to have patience with me. All this is new to me. It's something I never dreamed was possible for me."

"Baby girl, I'll give you all the time you need," Jeremy whispers.

"Thank you." Ashley steps back and smiles shyly. "Can we talk about kissing? All I know is what I've seen in movies."

Jeremy laughs. "You are assuming I'm an expert in that field?"

"Well, judging by the women flirting with you last night, you must be pretty good at it," Ashley says, blushing.

"Okay, okay. Let's not go there. What do you want to know?"

Chapter 26

JEREMY

Ashley takes a few minutes to ponder Jeremy's question. Then she says, "in the movies, it looks like there are different types of kisses."

"Let's walk while we talk." Ashley nods, and Jeremy takes her small hand in his larger one. "For me, there are four types of kisses," he begins. "The first one I call the hello kiss. It is a very innocent kiss, like the ones you give Devon. Then, depending on who it is, I sometimes use it on family and friends with a hug."

"That makes sense," Ashley says. "Is it ever on the lips?"

"For me, that depends on who it is. I never kiss the women in my family on the lips. If it is a personal friend, I might. But, knowing you, I can't think of any man you would kiss like that."

"You're probably right about that," Ashley replies. "What is the second type of kiss?"

"Well, I call it my I'd like to get to know you kiss. I've used it after a date if I liked the woman and wanted to see her again."

"Is that the way you kissed me last night?"

"Yeah, I guess it was. I really didn't plan or think about it. It just happened," Jeremy says, remembering the kiss. "Okay, let's stop for a minute, and let me explain something. You can't teach someone how to kiss. It's like you danced with me last night. You closed your eyes, and your body responded to my movements, following me on the dance floor. Everyone kisses differently, so it's more about the reaction. If you initiate the kiss and do the leading, the other person usually follows if they want to." Jeremy tells her.

"I think I understand," Ashley replies. "You have me curious now. What's the third kiss?"

Jeremy smiles at her. "Bear with me while I think about how to explain it." He drops her hand and walks a few feet away from Ashley with his back to her. He rubs his beard, releases his hair from the man bun, and shakes his head, so the wavy, dark brown locks lie on his shoulders. Then he turns to face Ashley.

She giggles and says, "you are really putting some serious thought into this, aren't you?"

Jeremy grins back at her. "Yeah, I am, because the third kiss involves more feelings."

"What kind of feelings?" Ashley asks innocently.

"By the third kiss, you want to know the other person deeper. The feelings can be intensely driven by desire, passion or need." Ashley looks confused. "You may desire the person sexually, or you want to show your love for them or need to feel close to them when the second type of kiss isn't enough." Ashley nods in understanding. "The third kiss is deeper. Most of the time, it involves French kissing. Do you know what that is?"

"Oh, of course. I've read about it and seen it in the movies," Ashley answers, rolling her eyes. "That's what people do when they make out, right?"

"Yes. The kiss becomes more personal between the two people at that point." Ashley looks away. Jeremy notices a tiny crease forming between her eyebrows and knows she is deep in thought.

I don't know what else to say, Jeremy thinks as he watches Ashley concentrate on his words. Then, finally, she turns and walks even farther away from him. Ashley bends, plucking a wildflower from the green grass, and lifts it to her nose. She inhales the scent several times before taking a deep breath and turning back toward Jeremy.

Ashley turns a bright shade of pink and says, "Jeremy, would you kiss me like that? I mean, if you don't mind. I want like to experience a kiss like that."

Ashley's words make his heart beat faster, and Jeremy closes the distance between them. "I want to, baby girl, but let's start with the second one first and progress from there."

Jeremy places his hands on her hips and gently pulls her to him. Ashley wraps her arms around his neck. He hugs her tightly and then pulls his head back to look at her. Ashley's blue eyes are soft and glowing, pulling Jeremy into a depth of feelings he's never felt. He gently kisses the tip of her nose as Ashley closes her eyes.

Jeremy lowers his lips to her perfect lips, watching her face as he does. When he touches her lips, his body immediately wants to move to the fourth type of kiss he hasn't mentioned yet. Jeremy struggles to keep his mind on the task at hand. Then he feels Ashley's lips respond to his.

The kiss lasts a few seconds. Then Jeremy moves his lips to Ashley's ear. He whispers, "are you sure you want to do this?"

"More than anything in the world," she whispers back.

Jeremy kisses a spot below Ashley's ear and then returns to her soft lips. The kiss begins as before, but now Ashley's kissing him back more. Jeremy tightens his hold on her waist, and his kiss becomes stronger. He brushes her lips with his tongue once and then again. Surprisingly, Ashley parts her lips, inviting him inside.

As Jeremy's tongue enters her mouth, his heart flip-flops in his chest. Ashley begins running her fingers through his hair and pulls his head down so their lips are joined in perfect union. She moans, making Jeremy's body react on its own. He moves one hand to her back and the other to her backside. He wants her to feel what she's causing to happen.

When Jeremy pulls his tongue back, Ashley moans his name. His tongue returns to the warm region of her mouth and begins exploring every inch of her mouth. When he's finished, he lets Ashley do the same. The kissing continues for several minutes until Jeremy can't take it any longer. He lifts his head, pulls away from her lips, and backs away. Jeremy places his hands on his knees and tries to catch his breath.

After several deep breaths, Jeremy looks up to find Ashley gingerly touching her lips and tears filling her eyes. Then, concerned he may have hurt her, he asks, "are you okay?"

Chapter 27

ASHLEY

Her lips feel somewhat puffy and tender. When Jeremy asks if she is okay, Ashley smiles and replies, "that was the most exciting and wonderful thing I have ever experienced in my life." She watches as Jeremy stands upright and adjusts himself before returning to stand before her. "Did I do okay?"

Jeremy reaches out, taking Ashley's face in both hands. "Baby girl, I don't think I need to answer that question. I will say this, though. I definitely do not need to explain the fourth type of kiss to you." Jeremy clears his throat. "Ashley, I am very honored you chose me to be the first man you kissed."

Ashley looks into Jeremy's teary eyes and knows he is being honest with her. "Ah, do you think we could do it again soon?" She blushes.

"Is now soon enough?" Jeremy asks, lowering his lips to hers.

After several more kisses than Ashley could sense were getting more intense by the minute, she says," I think we better go back. We've probably missed lunch, and I bet Devon wonders where you are." Jeremy agrees, and the pair walk back to the line shack holding hands.

"Jeremy," Ashley says when they reach the cabin. "I think I need a woman to talk to. Would it upset you if I talked to G?"

"No, but you can always talk to me. I hope you know that."

"I do, but I think I need a woman's opinion and guidance."

Jeremy squeezes her hand. "I understand, Ashley. I wish I had had a man to talk to when things began happening in my life. G tried to help, and so did my grandfather. Will you come to the house for dinner?"

"Yes, I'll be there," she replies, kissing Jeremy's lips softly. She watches as he smiles and walks away.

Ashley walks to the side of the cabin, picks up her cap and gloves, and returns to her work. Unable to concentrate, she sits down and contemplates the kissing between herself and Jeremy. The kissing was so wonderful, but the feelings that happened while it was going on were confusing, to say the least. Her body got extremely hot. It was a different type of hot than she had experienced working out in the scorching sun all day. Places in her tingled and became damp.

Then there was Jeremy's reaction. His body got hot with sweat, and he got breathless at times. But, while they held each other tightly, his body showed excitement. That never happened when he was holding her in bed after her nightmares. I'm so confused. Maybe I can talk to G tonight or tomorrow. After a while, Ashley returns to her work. I must be finished before tomorrow morning when the workers arrive. We have a full day's work ahead of us then.

Everyone wants an update on Ashley's project during dinner. She tells them the work is on schedule, but she needs 100 gallons of water and a larger generator to test the cistern before an electrician comes on Tuesday. Hank tells Ashley everything she needs is on the ranch. He will contact Tyler in the morning and deliver it to the line shack.

After dinner, Ashley says, "G, can we go for a walk?"

"Of course, my dear," she replies, noticing Jeremy brushes Ashley's cheek tenderly after taking Devon out of his high chair.

The two women walk down into the valley, discussing the multitude of wildflowers as they go. "Ashley, you didn't ask me to walk with you to talk about the flowers, did you?"

"G, I don't want to make you uncomfortable. I asked Jeremy's permission to talk to you. But, unfortunately, I don't have a woman to talk to, and there are things I don't understand."

G nods. "Ashley, I'm thrilled you feel comfortable talking to me, and we can talk about anything and everything you wish to. But I must warn you, I'm no expert if this is about men."

Ashley laughs. "No, this is about women." Ashley is honest with G. She has never been with or kissed a man. Because of her trust issues, she never even considered a relationship with a man. Ashley tells G about kissing Jeremy and the feeling in her body without going into great detail.

G explains the feeling is a natural reaction a woman has when she finds a man very attractive. Ashley listens as G says it is up to the woman how deep the woman wants to get into a relationship. It is also the woman's choice if she wants to give in to her feelings. Let no one pressure you into doing something you don't want to or are not comfortable doing, G tells her.

"You are starting to care about Jeremy, aren't you?" G asks.

Ashley contemplates the question for a few seconds before answering. "I think so. I trust him with some things, but not others. I'm afraid he will turn away from me when he learns about my past."

"You need to give Jeremy a little more credit than that. He didn't turn away from Devon's mother when she told him she was pregnant. Jeremy loved her to a point, but it wasn't the forever love we all desire. He doesn't realize it, but he's searching for that kind of love. Jeremy's a thirty-year-old kid at heart, but that kind of love will make him the man and father he is meant to be. When he finds the right woman, it will probably scare him at first, and he may run away from it. But he will realize later that he needs and wants the love that woman will give him."

G pauses and looks out over the valley. "Are you that woman, Ashley? I don't know if you are or not. I just hope Jeremy finds the woman he is meant to share his life with. Devon will play an enormous part in Jeremy's decision when the time comes."

"Thank you for your honesty, G. I never intended to be friends with Jeremy. I just planned to do what I was hired to do and then return to Vegas. But, now, I want to be his friend and get to know him," Ashley says.

G pats Ashley's hand. "Life happens, and what is will be. So take things one day at a time and don't rush into anything."

"Hey, are the two of you going to talk all night?" Jeremy yells from above. "I brought flashlights. It's getting dark, and I need to get you back to your houses safely."

"Sweet Jeremy. Always looking out for his elderly grandmother," G comments.

"Elderly is the last thing I would call you, G," Jeremy laughs as he walks up. He helps her off the boulder and kisses her cheek. G pats him on the chest in return.

"Give me a flashlight, Jeremy. Then you can walk Ashley back to the cabin," G says, reaching out her hand.

"Yes, ma'am." Jeremy hands G a flashlight. Then he and Ashley watch her walk away. Next, Jeremy bows to Ashley. "Madam, your personal bodyguard is here to guide you to your home, away from home. I would much prefer it was to the bedroom next door to mine, though." Ashley swats him on the arm and giggles. "I love your laugh, baby girl," Jeremy says as he stands and offers her his hand.

"May I ask how your talk went?" Jeremy asks.

"It went well. I understand things better now. Don't worry, I didn't give any details," Ashley tells him with a smile.

"I wasn't worried about it. I trust you, Ashley."

When they reach the cabin, Jeremy pulls Ashley into his arms, kissing her deeply once. "See you tomorrow, baby girl," he says, walking away.

Chapter 28

JEREMY

After putting Devon down for the night, Jeremy climbs into bed, but sleep evades him. Instead, he stares at the ceiling, reliving kissing Ashley. For someone that had never kissed a man, she caught on quickly; he thinks. And boy, did she catch on. I have never enjoyed a kiss so much, nor has one ever turned me on like that. The feelings and emotions I felt during and after those kisses are like nothing I have ever felt. The inner voice interrupts because you're falling in love with her. No, I'm not, Jeremy declares. It's just been a while since I was with a woman. Maybe I better do something about that this week. Yeah, right, the voice says. You can try, but only one woman is in your blood now.

Suddenly, Ashley pops into his mind and not in a good way. Jeremy jumps out of bed, grabs his keys, and runs to the line shack wearing only his boxers. He hears the faint screams before he even reaches the cabin. Jeremy opens the door, not bothering to close it. He rushes to Ashley's bedside and climbs in next to her.

"Ashley. Ashley. Wake up, baby girl," he whispers, pulling her to him.

"Jeremy?"

"I'm here, baby."

Ashley shivers. "Jeremy, something is going to happen soon. I can feel it. The nightmares are becoming more frequent. There's something in my subconscious trying to come out."

"What can I do to help?" Jeremy whispers.

"Exactly what you're doing now," Ashley whispers back.

Ashley was resting comfortably when Jeremy left to go back to his bedroom. He checked on Devon and then climbed back into his bed. Exhausted, Jeremy fell into a deep sleep and dreamed of Ashley crouched on a floor with a faceless man standing over her with a belt in his hand.

The following morning, a sudden bounce of the bed wakes Jeremy. He opens his eyes to find Devon staring down at him. "Papa, pee, pee." Jeremy gets up and takes Devon to the bathroom.

When they return, Jeremy puts Devon back in his little bed. "Devon, did G take you out of bed?" Devon shakes his head and shows his papa how he climbed over the rails and out of bed. "Oh, for Pete's sake," Jeremy says. "What do I do now?" Devon giggles and climbs back into his bed.

Jeremy dresses Devon and himself. He sends Devon to the dining room. Then he calls Michelle, Devon's maternal grandmother, to inquire if she has this problem. Michelle laughs and explains the steps she took to eliminate the problem.

"I need to go and take care of an urgent matter. Ashley, if you don't need me, I'd like to drive to Jackson Hole. I heard they are building a ski ramp," Jeremy says, sitting for breakfast.

"Jeremy, by all means, go. Everything here is fine," Ashley replies.

After breakfast, Jeremy drives into town and buys items to make Devon's bed escape-proof. Next, he heads to view the new ski ramp. The owner of the resort is pleased to see Jeremy. They tour the new natural slope. Jeremy is an experienced skier with a name that can draw potential business to the resort. So the resort owner offers Jeremy the opportunity to be the first to use the slope once it snows. Jeremy accepts, but only if he can do the photographs to advertise the ramp. The owner agrees, and they settle on a price. Jeremy can't wait to tell Ashley when he gets home.

On the way back to the house, Jeremy pulls over to remove the flyer someone put under his windshield wiper. Since he hadn't noticed it before, Jeremy didn't know if it happened in town or at the resort. He tosses it into his bag of supplies and continues his drive, reaching the house at dinnertime.

After dinner, Jeremy and Ashley work on Devon's bed. Jeremy tells Ashley about the new ski ramp and the owner's invitation to let Jeremy be the first to try it out. Ashley takes the opportunity to learn about skiing and Jeremy's background in the sport. He explains he enjoys all types of skiing and snowboarding. He wasn't good enough for the Olympics, but he won many worldwide awards.

When they finish, Jeremy throws the bag with the flyer into the trash and walks Ashley home. They sit on the porch swing, watch a storm move over the mountains, and kiss a lot. The intensity builds and builds. Jeremy is a perfect gentleman, although his body demands release. He finally tells Ashley he needs to put Devon to bed and leaves. Jeremy doesn't tell her the real reason he's leaving is to take care of himself in the shower.

Chapter 29

ASHLEY

The electrician arrives at 9:00 am. He, along with Ashley and the workers, begins work immediately. The solar panels are installed on the roof of the enclosed room, housing the cistern by lunch. By dinner, everything is hooked up and ready for testing. Jeremy, Devon, G, Hank, Ida and Tyler arrive for the test. Everything goes according to Ashley's plan. Ashley starts the generator. The water from the cistern flows through a filtration system. Then, water is pumped to the cold water faucets or an instant water heater.

Everyone claps with excitement. There's no need to haul five-gallon bottles of water to the line shack. The water will no longer need to be heated on the propane stove or fireplace. Ashley explains power from the solar panels will replace the generator. Rainwater will be collected by the gutters on the cabin and flow into the cistern. She also explains the heating system she designed to prevent the water in the cistern from freezing during the long, cold winters. It, too, will be powered by solar panels.

After the demonstration, the electrician and workers leave for the day. Rain is predicted for the following day, so the workers will have the day off. Everyone except Ashley and Jeremy head back to the house.

"Baby girl, I'm so proud of you," Jeremy says, pulling Ashley into his arms. "But I'm disappointed too."

"Why?" Ashley asks.

"There's less reason for you to come to the house to bathe or eat."

Ashley smiles. "But there's more reason for you to come here."

"You are so right," Jeremy says, kissing her deeply. Too deeply, in fact. "We better go up to the house for dinner," he says, backing away from Ashley. She nods in understanding and takes his hand.

As everyone sits down for dinner, Hank places a piece of paper beside G's plate. "I got it out of the trash," he tells her.

Jeremy glances at it. "It was on my windshield yesterday. I didn't look at it. What's it for?"

G reads over it quickly and says, "it's a tent revival in town this week. I haven't been to one in years. It sounds interesting, so I may go." She lays it on the table between herself and Ashley.

Ashley glances at it, picks it up, and studies it for a few seconds. The flyer has a picture of the preacher. Then she turns ghostly pale and jumps up, turning her chair over. She quickly runs from the room with the flyer in her hand. Ashley removes her phone from her pocket in the living room and dials a number.

"Ashley, are you okay?" Jeremy asks, having followed her. She points to the phone in her ear.

"Sadie, it's Ashley. I am fine. I'm in Wyoming. Sadie, I need you. He's here. Okay. Okay. Let me know when you're on your way. Thanks."

"Ashley, what's going on? You have me worried," Jeremy says.

Ashley holds up the flyer. "My father," is all she can say before Jeremy catches her falling to the floor.

When she wakes, Ashley is lying on the sofa, surrounded by everyone. Jeremy is sitting beside her, holding her hand.

"Here, drink this," G says, holding a glass to Ashley. "Don't ask what it is. Just sip it slowly."

Ashley sits up with Jeremy's help and takes a sip. The liquid is the same color as Jeremy's hair and burns her throat as she swallows it.

"I guess I owe you an explanation," Ashley says. "I will spare you the details of the long, sordid story right now. But this man is my father, who abandoned me when I was sixteen."

"Your name differs from his," G says.

"Yes, he changed his name because the police in our town wanted to talk to him about a potential crime. But, unfortunately, they could never find him. The woman I called is Sadie Williams, a detective there. She will contact the police department here and have him picked up. Sadie will call me when she's on her way here." Ashley drinks the rest of the warm liquid. "Jeremy, will you take me to the cabin? I want to sleep here tonight, and I need some things."

"Do you want something to eat first?" Jeremy asks.

"I can't eat, but may take another drink when we return."

Chapter 30

JEREMY

Jeremy walks Ashley to the cabin, respecting her privacy and not talking. When they are inside the cabin, he asks," what can I do to help you?"

Ashley sits down on her bed. "Do you remember I said something would happen?" Jeremy nods and sits beside her. "I guess this is it. Jeremy, I'm going to sleep in my bedroom at the house. I will probably have nightmares every night. I told you something is trying to enter my mind. Hopefully, this will cause it to happen. If you hear me having a nightmare, please don't wake me. I need to have the full nightmare."

"Can I sleep with you so I can be sure you don't hurt yourself?" he asks, taking her hand in his.

"I would like that," Ashley replies. "The rest I'll figure out when Sadie calls to tell me when they will question him. Let's get my things and get back to the house. I could really use another drink."

After returning to the house and getting Ashley settled in her bedroom, Jeremy and Ashley go to the living room. The house is quiet, and everyone is elsewhere. Jeremy pours Ashley and himself a drink and sits beside her on the sofa. He hands her the glass, puts his arm around her shoulders, and pulls her to him. Ashley raises the glass to her lips. Her hand shakes so badly that she spills some of the bourbon on her pants.

Jeremy takes the glass from her, sitting it on a table as tears begin to slide down her cheeks. Jeremy sets his glass down and stands. He wraps Ashley's arms around his neck before lifting her. He carries her to her bedroom, sits on the bed, and lowers her into his lap.

"Cry, baby girl. Let it out," Jeremy whispers in Ashley's ear. She leans her face against his beard and sobs for a very long time. Ashley is exhausted by the time the sobbing ceases. Jeremy lies her down on the bed and goes to find G.

"G, can I move Devon's bed into your room for a few nights?" Jeremy asks.

"Of course. Jeremy, right now, Ashley needs to be your priority. You're the only real friend she has in this world," G answers. He nods, goes to his bedroom, and moves Devon's bed. Then he begins to work.

First, Jeremy looks through Ashley's bag, searching for a gown or pajamas instead, finding an old tattered teddy bear. Finding none, he gets one of his t-shirts. Then, Jeremy turns back the bedcovers on his bed because Jeremy has a mattress cover because of Devon. Next, he goes to Ashley, where he carefully removes her clothes and slips his t-shirt on her. Finally, he carries her to his bed, placing the teddy bear in her arms.

Jeremy tells Devon goodnight and instructs him to be a good boy for G. He returns to his bedroom, where a peacefully sleeping Ashley lies. Jeremy strips down to his boxers and climbs beside her, pulling her into his arms. As he holds Ashley close, Jeremy remembers the expression and color on Ashley's face when she recognized her father. Hopefully, this situation will come to a head soon, and Ashley's nightmare can end, he thinks.

Chapter 31

ASHLEY

The following morning, Ashley wakes up, confused and alone. She's not in her bed. She's in Jeremy's bed. I don't think I had a nightmare, she thinks, spying the tattered teddy bear. She hugs it tightly and then hears a moan from the bathroom. Ashley hears the shower running and decides Jeremy must be taking a hot shower. Next, she hears her name in a louder voice, barely distinguishable over the running water.

Ashley gets up and walks to the bathroom door, concerned Jeremy might be in pain and calling her. She quickly stops halfway into the room. Ashley can see Jeremy from the side. He is standing in the walk-in shower with one hand against the wall. His head is leaning back with his wet long brown hair lying against his shoulders and back. Jeremy's chest moves rapidly with each breath. His other hand is below his waist, with his arm moving up and down. His knees are slightly bent.

Mesmerized by the sight of the handsome, muscular man, Ashley watches. She knows what he's doing. She read about it in books. Ashley starts to back out of the room but hears Jeremy call her name. His arm stops moving as he tries to catch his breath. Suddenly Jeremy's head turns slightly, and he looks directly into her eyes. Feeling guilty for being caught watching, Ashley hurries back to the bed, crawling under the covers and pulling them over her head. She hears the water turn off and holds her breath.

The silence in the room is almost too much for Ashley to bear. Perhaps Jeremy left, she thinks. Suddenly the comforter and sheet are jerked off of Ashley, leaving her lying on her back, covered only by Jeremy's t-shirt. Jeremy gets into bed beside her. He lies on his side, leaning on his elbow. His free hand strokes her cheek and then trails down her neck to the collar of the t-shirt. Then, across the collar to the other side of Ashley's neck and cheek.

"I'm sorry, Jeremy," Ashley whispers, turning a bright shade of pink.

"What are you sorry for?" he asks, playing with a strand of her hair, tickling the outside of her ear as he does it.

"For, for, for interrupting your private time," she stammers.

"You must know how much I want you," Jeremy whispers. "I'm willing to wait until you're ready, but it's time you got a little sample of what's waiting for you." Jeremy leans over, and his kisses follow the trail his fingers made. Next, his tongue softly strokes the outside of Ashley's ear. Jeremy sucks on her earlobe and bites gently as his hand slides across her stomach before moving over her chest.

"Jeremy," Ashley moans. "Please don't stop."

"I have to," he replies as he pulls away. "I don't want to, but I have to."

"Why?"

"Because you don't trust me enough yet to give yourself to me fully. Your body wants to give in, but your heart and mind are not ready."

"At least kiss me," Ashley murmurs.

"Gladly," Jeremy replies, giving her his most passionate kiss. Then, he pulls away, climbs out of bed, and begins dressing. "You slept well last night."

"I did." Ashley picks up the teddy bear. "This was mine when I was a little girl. I thought it might help me remember what I need to. Maybe tonight. Why am I in your bed, Jeremy?"

"It has a mattress cover for when Devon gets into bed with me. I thought this might be the best to sleep if you have one of those dreadful nights where you wake up all wet."

Ashley's phone rings. "It's Sadie. Don't leave, Jeremy," Ashley says when Jeremy walks toward the door. "Hi, Sadie. Okay, that sounds great. I'll be there. I need this, Sadie. You know that better than anyone. Just give me a chance. Okay. I'll see you there." Ashley hangs up. "Sadie is flying in tonight. The police will pick my father up in the morning. I need to be there at 9:00 am."

"What can I do?" Jeremy asks.

"Let me think about it, and we'll talk later." Jeremy nods, leaving Ashley in the room to dress.

Rain pours from the sky all day, making the day dark and dreary, matching Ashley's mood. So she stays in her bedroom most of the day staring out the window. Finally, refusing to leave the room for dinner, Hank brings Ashley a tray.

After setting the tray down, Hank hugs her and says, "do what your heart tells you to do, sweetheart." Then he leaves, and tears come to Ashley's eyes. Jeremy knocks on the door and enters without waiting for an invitation. He walks over to Ashley and wipes her tears away.

"I'm so tired of crying, Jeremy. Who knew a person's body could produce so many tears?"

"I know, baby girl, but now it's time to put on that armor you've been wearing for so long and fight. I'll stand beside you, behind you, or fight the damn battle myself. Just tell me what you want me to do because you will not do this without me."

"Sit with me while I eat. I have a few requests for you. If you say no, I'll understand and still respect you the next day," Ashley says, winking at Jeremy. He smiles, and they sit at the table. Ashley talks while she eats.

"I may ask you to do something you could get in trouble for afterward."

"Okay, I think I look pretty cute in black and white stripes," Jeremy replies.

Ashley rolls her eyes. "You look pretty cute in anything and nothing, Jeremy Marsh. I can make that statement after this morning."

"Well, I would like to hear more about your opinion of my body, but we have business to attend to," Jeremy says as he wiggles his eyebrows.

"First, I want to wear the clothes you bought me for our date. I will feel you with me by wearing them, bringing comfort and strength." Jeremy nods. "Second, I want you to sleep with me again tonight. This will be my last chance to bring out the memory I need to put at least part of this behind me. Remember, don't wake me up," Ashley tells him.

"I'm okay with that," Jeremy replies, scooting his chair closer, so his knees are touching hers.

"Third, I may need you to run interference for me. Probably not with Sadie, but with the local police." Ashley pauses. "Fourth, please don't hate me after tomorrow."

"I could never hate you." Jeremy reaches over, taking her hand in his and squeezing it tightly.

"I can't be sure. But you will find out about my ugly past and why I haven't been able to trust anyone."

"I'm going to be very selfish and say I hope this brings us closer."

"I would like that very much," Ashley states, and for the first time, she initiates a kiss. It is she that takes control, demanding entrance to Jeremy's mouth with the tip of her tongue on his lips. It is Ashley pulling him closer to her, wanting to feel his warmth against her body. Jeremy lets her control everything, partly because he knows she needs it and partly because it excites him.

Without breaking the kiss, Ashley eases into Jeremy's lap. The two kiss deeply and more passionately than ever before for several minutes. Finally, Jeremy ends the make-out session by declaring he must shower.

During the night, Ashley's faint voice wakes Jeremy. She is murmuring, and he can't make out the words. She isn't covered in sweat but curls into a fetal position clutching the old teddy bear. Ashley whimpers several times. True to his word, Jeremy doesn't wake her but watches her closely. Finally, he feels her calm and relaxes her body.

Chapter 32

JEREMY

Jeremy has been watching Ashley sleep since sunrise. He marvels at the beauty of the woman lying in his arms. Ashley's jet-black hair spreads across her pillow and his shoulder. Her long, black eyelashes fan out across her creamy soft cheeks. Ashley's perfect lips are slightly curved at the corners. Her arm is draped over Jeremy's chest, and one leg covers both of his.

You're in love with her, the inner voice says. No, no, no. I care about her, Jeremy's mind replies. Liar, the voice says. Man up and do something about it before you lose her. It is obvious she has feelings for you. Oh, shut up.

Ashley stirs and opens her eyes. "Are you watching me sleep?"

"I was. Do you have a problem with it?"

Ashley rolls over on top of Jeremy, so she is straddling him. "No. No, I don't. Are you ticklish?" she asks, moving her hands down to his sides. Then she tries to tickle Jeremy.

At first, he fights the urge to laugh, but Ashley is relentless. Jeremy rolls her over and is now on top of her. He grabs her wrists, pinning them above her head with one hand. Jeremy can tell she's expecting him to tickle her, but instead, he lowers his head and places tiny kisses along her jaw. Then he moves down to her ears and neck.

"Papa!" Devon yells as he jumps on the bed.

"That ends that," Jeremy whispers in Ashley's ears.

"Lele, why you in papa's bed?" Devon asks with a perplexed look on his little face.

"Lele was trying to tickle me like this," Jeremy declares, rolling off Ashley. He pins Devon down and tickles him. Little boy laughter fills the room.

"Pee pee, papa," Devon says in between giggles. Jeremy lets him up, and Devon runs to the bathroom.

"You dreamed last night," Jeremy whispers to Ashley.

"I know. I got the message," she replies as Devon jumps back on the bed.

Jeremy paces the floor in the living room, waiting for Ashley. He's just as nervous as he was for their first date, but this is different. Very different, and it makes him uncomfortable.

Ashley walks into the room wearing the clothes Jeremy bought her. She's just as beautiful as she was for their date, but today, there is a hardness. Ashley's jet-black hair is in a ponytail. It's as if the dress is a suit of armor, and Ashley is ready for the fight of her life. Everyone hugs her but says nothing. What could they say, Jeremy thinks? Only he has an idea of what the day will bring.

Chapter 33

ASHLEY

S adie is waiting by the front door of the police station as Ashley and Jeremy walk up the steps. Ashley hugs Sadie tightly and then introduces Jeremy. Sadie leads them to a small, windowless room.

"Ashley, your father is in an interrogation room. He's been read his rights and waived his right to an attorney. However, he is being very obnoxious and mean. The house is old and rundown, but still standing. I have a team out there now checking the place for blood. I should hear from them soon. Are you ready to get started?" Ashley nods.

Sadie leads Ashley and Jeremy into a small room with a large window. Sadie introduces a man and woman as two Jackson detectives. Ashley goes to the window and stares at the man she hasn't seen in ten years.

Her father is almost bald. He has gained a great deal of weight over the years. His suit coat is stretched to the max to cover the pot belly. Her father is leaning back in the chair, humming a gospel song Ashley recognizes.

"Is he handcuffed?" Ashley asks.

"There's been no need to yet. We'll see how it goes when Sadie gets in there," the male detective answers.

Ashley turns, observing the small room. A table with two chairs is next to the window. Recording equipment takes up most of the table, but there are also pens and legal pads. At the end of the table, far from the door, lies a police nightstick.

"Ashley, are you ready?" Sadie asks.

"Yes, let's send this bastard to hell," Ashley replies.

"Do you know something you need to share with me?" Sadie asks.

"Let's say it's my ace in the hole," Ashley answers.

Sadie enters the room with Ashley's father, Rev. James Wilson, and introduces herself. Sadie starts by informing Rev. Wilson that she knows his real name is Jonathan Ramsey. Rev. Wilson vehemently denies he's Ramsey. Next, Sadie moves on to the reason Ramsey is there. She needs to question him about his wife's disappearance ten years ago. Ramsey again denies the name change. Finally, he slams his meaty fist on the metal table and says he doesn't understand why he's there and wants to leave.

Once the fist hits the table, the male and female detectives enter the room and place handcuffs on Ramsey. Then they and Sadie exit the room as Sadie's phone rings. Back inside the small room, Sadie answers it, listening to whoever called. Finally, she thanks them and hangs up.

"Ashley, they found traces of blood in the kitchen. Someone worked to clean it up, but they didn't get it all. I'm going back in to talk to him."

"No, I'm going," Ashley says quietly.

"I can't let you do that," Sadie says.

"You can and you will because we both know I'm the only one that can break him," Ashley replies. "All this is being recorded, and I'm not the police, so can they can use everything he says in court?"

Jeremy speaks for the first time since entering the room. "Sadie, Ashley needs this. I've been with her during and after her nightmares. I believe this is the only way to get them to end for her."

Sadie takes a deep breath. "Okay, Ashley, but if it gets out of hand, I will come in and stop it."

"I would like the male detective to leave," Ashley says. The man opens the door to go out, and Jeremy steps in that direction. "No, Jeremy. I need you to stay. Please."

"Okay, baby girl." Jeremy steps back to where he was.

Ashley steps in front of him. She kisses him on the cheek and says, "thank you. Please distract them for a minute, and no matter what happens, do not let them in until I'm ready." Ashley takes two steps back. Jeremy pretends to get strangled. Sadie and the female detective walk over to assist him while Ashley slides the nightstick under her dress. She blows Jeremy a kiss and walks to the door as he regains his breath and smiles.

Chapter 34

JEREMY

The door to the interrogation room opens. Jeremy watches Ashley calmly enter the room, closing the door behind her. Ramsey yells at her to remove the handcuffs, but Ashley ignores him. Instead, she bends down in front of the glass. Jeremy knows Ashley is laying the nightstick down where it can't be seen. When Ashley straightens up, she looks into the one-way mirror, touching her heart. Jeremy knows it's her signal that she feels him with her.

Ashley takes a deep breath. Jeremy's heart swells with pride as he watches his warrior, his baby girl. "My baby girl," he whispers. Before his eyes, Ashley transforms from a five-foot-seven-inch woman to a seven-foot giant ready to meet her demons head-on. Jeremy positions himself between the detectives and the door leading into the room.

"Well, at least the detectives are getting better looking," Ramsey says snidely.

"I'm not a detective," Ashley says coldly as she turns around to face her father on the opposite side of the metal table. "Don't you recognize me?" Ramsey shakes his head. "Let me remind you." Ashley pulls the scrunchie from her hair, letting her black locks flow to her shoulders and back. She leans over the table.

"Ashley?" Ramsey says in astonishment. Ashley nods. She can immediately tell he has forgotten about his actions being recorded. "You look just like your whore of a mother."

"My mother wasn't a whore, old man. But I'm going to let that comment slide for a little while. Then we'll circle back to it."

"What do you want?" Ramsey asks hatefully.

As Jeremy and the two women detectives watch on, Ashley asks, "where's my brother?"

Ramsey laughs. "Your brother? After all this time, you want to know about your brother?"

"Did you kill him?"

"No, of course, I didn't kill him," Ramsey huffs. "How dare you think me, a man of God, could do such a thing?"

"Man of God? That's another thing we'll reevaluate. Now, how would I know what happened? I went to bed with him beside me; the next morning, he was gone. You wouldn't answer me when I asked where he was."

"The truth is, I couldn't raise two kids alone. There was a couple at the church that couldn't have kids. They were moving to Wyoming, so I gave your brother to them to raise as their own. They moved a week later."

"What were their names so I can verify your story?" Ashley demands.

"Harrison. Bill and Janet Harrison," Ramsey yells. "I want to leave!"

"No, we're just getting started," Ashley replies. Although Jeremy can't see her face, he knows a mask of hatred hides her beauty. "Where's my mother?"

"Your mother?" Ramsey laughs. His voice is shaking from anger. "I told you, then she left. That whore probably ran off with a man she met at church."

"My mother wasn't a whore. She worked hard to raise your two kids. She cleaned, cooked, and did laundry almost every day. She taught Sunday School every Sunday and led the Women's Bible study group every Wednesday. So when did she have time to be with another man?" Ashley asks.

By now, Ramsey's face is blood red with anger. "How should I know?" he replies.

"I'll tell you what I know. The morning she supposedly left, you were burning something in the burn barrel. I watched you. When you left for the church, a downpour came and put the fire out. I got a stick and poked through the ashes. What did I find? My mother's clothes. You were burning her clothes. I went into the house and looked at the suitcases. None were missing."

Ashley walks over to the window and bends over. Jeremy knows she is picking up the nightstick, and he wonders if Ashley will hit her father with it. Instead, she walks to the table and hits it with the nightstick. Jeremy sees the table vibrate from the strike. The two women detectives move toward the door, but Jeremy blocks their way. They move back to the window slowly.

Ramsey jumps when the nightstick hits the table, but he sits back in the chair with a smug expression on his face. "I don't know what to tell you, Ashley. She left."

"Okay, then. Shall we continue?" Ashley asks.

"Whatever," Ramsey replies.

"This morning, the police searched the house. Guess what they found, old man. They found blood in the kitchen and areas where someone tried to clean it up with bleach. I remember the powerful odor of bleach when I work up that morning."

"Ashley, Ashley, Ashley," Ramsey says. "That doesn't prove a thing. You know I went deer hunting with some men from church."

"Animal blood doesn't react to the chemicals they use." Ashley slams the nightstick down on the table again. "Let me continue. I heard the fight you and my mother had that night. You were hitting her. She was praying and asking you to stop. Then, finally, she told you she was hurt. But you didn't stop, did you? So then she told you she was leaving and taking my brother and me with her."

"So we argued," Ramsey says. "Parents do that all the time." A snug look replaces the angry look on his face. He smiles at Ashley.

Ashley strikes the nightstick on the table again. "Why did my mother tell you she was leaving?" Ramsey shrugs his shoulder. "She told you she saw you fondling a twelve-year-old girl in your office. She was going to report you to the police and then leave."

"Oh hell," Jeremy says aloud. That was the memory that kept evading Ashley. He looks at the two women in the room with him. Horror is written all over their faces.

Ramsey sits straight in his chair and looks at Ashley with pure hate in his eyes. "You dreamed that. You are just inventing a story to get me into trouble."

Again, the nightstick slams into the table. "You didn't let me finish. I heard all the arguing. I heard you hit my mother. She begged you to stop, and I heard her praying. Finally, I heard a loud bang, and there was total silence except for your heavy breathing. Then you said, and I quote, "oh God, what have I done? "."

Ramsey jumps from his chair, panic on his face. "It was an accident, Ashley. I didn't mean to strike her." Ramsey begins sobbing. "She fell and wouldn't get up. She wasn't breathing."

Ashley slams the nightstick on the table again. "Where is she?" Ashley yells.

"In the garden. I buried her in the garden." Ramsey falls into his chair, lays his head on the table, and sobs.

Stunned, Jeremy notices Sadie reach for her phone and dials a number. All she says is the garden and hangs up. Then she makes her way to the door. "Let me out, Jeremy."

"I can't do that," he replies. "Ashley hasn't given me the signal that she's finished."

"My God," the other detective says. "What else can there be?" Jeremy and the two women look at each other when suddenly, the nightstick hits the table again.

"Shut up, old man!" Ashley screams.

"I, I don't know what else you want from me," Ramsey stammers, still sobbing, with his head on the table.

"This isn't for you. This is for me," Ashley says. "What happened after my mother and brother were gone? Do you remember?" Ramsey looks up at her. "You beat me every Monday night. Remember? I couldn't go to school for two days, but you made sure I was well enough to go to church with you on Sunday, didn't you?"

"I had to protect you."

"Protect me? Protect me?" Ashley states in a low voice. "Oh, yeah, I remember now. You wanted to protect from what was it you called it? I believe you called it the face of evil. Old man, you were the evil for ten years of my life." Ashley pauses. "Do you remember what happened on the night of my sixteenth birthday? You forgot that, didn't you? Well, let me remind you."

Jeremy and the women watch in stunned silence as Ashley turns her back to her father. She pulls her dress off, holding it in front of her to hide her private area and breasts. Ashley turns her head, looking at her father over her shoulder.

"Look, old man! Look at the scars your belt buckle left behind," Ashley demands. Then she slowly turns around and says, "you left the next morning. So when I struggled to get out of bed, I couldn't. The blood from my body had soaked into the sheets and dried. So when I tried to get up, the sheet pulled away from my skin, making me bleed all over again."

Tears fill the eyes of Jeremy, Sadie and the other woman flowing down their cheeks.

"I laid there for three days. Then, finally, a nice policewoman came to check on me because the school notified the police I wasn't in school."

"That was you, wasn't it, Sadie?" Jeremy asks. Sadie can only nod her head.

"I was dehydrated, starving, and too weak to move from the blood loss. The gracious lady wrapped me in the sheets and took me to the emergency room. Unfortunately, my wounds were infected by then. I wouldn't have lived much longer." Ramsey looks down at the table.

"Look at me!" Ashley screams. When Ramsey doesn't, she picks up the nightstick and slams it into the metal table so hard she leaves a dent. "Look at me, I said!" Ramsey looks up. "You left me with a house six months behind on the mortgage. The utilities hadn't been paid for three. There was no food or money in the house."

"I didn't know what else to do," Ramsey says.

"Well, I know what I'm going to do. I will ensure your names and pictures are blasted throughout the United States in all the available media resources. I'll even pay for it if I file for bankruptcy. I want you to wake up every day wondering if it will be your last day on earth. I want you to wonder if a prison inmate will kill you, a parent of a child you harmed, or if your wife will poison you."

Anger reddens Ramsey's face. "I can't believe you'd be that cruel."

"I can and will be. Go to hell, father!" Ashley says quietly. She turns and nods at the window.

Jeremy steps back from the door as the door opens. Sadie and the other woman rush into Ramsey. Ashley, head held high, walks out of the room and into Jeremy's waiting arms. He holds her tightly.

"Jeremy, I think I broke my arm," Ashley whispers. He releases her and steps back. He takes the dress Ashley has been clutching in front of her and carefully pulls it over her head.

"Let's go, my precious baby girl," Jeremy says, holding her close to his side as he leads her to his SUV.

Chapter 35

ASHLEY

The ride back to the ranch is quiet. Ashley is exhausted and doses off and on. Getting treated for a broken arm at the hospital took a while. Ashley is almost asleep when the doctor puts a brace on her arm. She remembers Jeremy putting her in his lap and laying her head on his shoulder before driving home. Ashley wakes up when they reach the ranch enough to know Jeremy carried her to his bedroom. He undressed her, laid her on the bed, and climbed beside her.

The following morning, the movement of the bed awakens Ashley. She opens her eyes slowly, looking at the ceiling. She turns her head and finds Devon asleep, curled up between her and Jeremy. This is the way I wish things could be, Ashley thinks. Her inner voice says it could be possible if you open your heart to Jeremy. Perhaps I can now that he knows all my ugly secrets. But, of course, it will depend on his reaction to what he's learned.

Ashley feels a hand touch the top of her head. "Good morning, baby girl," Jeremy's voice says quietly. "How did you sleep?"

"I slept better than I've slept in years," Ashley replies.

"It looks like we have an intruder."

"I prefer to call if a visitor," Ashley says with a grin. "Why does my arm hurt?" Then, not wanting to disturb a sleeping Devon, she raises the arm slowly. "What happened to me?"

"You don't remember?" Jeremy asks. Ashley turns her head, looking at Jeremy, and shakes her head. "You broke it the last time you smashed the nightstick into the table. You hit the steel table so hard you dented it."

Devon turns on his side, facing Ashley, and opens his eyes. "Lele," he says. "Can I call you mama since you and papa sleep together?"

Jeremy's jaw flies open, but Ashley smiles at the little boy. "Sweetheart, that's a conversation for you and your papa when alone.

"Okay, Lele. Sleep now," Devon says, closing his eyes and dozing off.

Jeremy turns on his side, facing Devon and Ashley. He reaches past Devon and brushes Ashley's cheek with his fingertips. "I do not know where that came from," he whispers, "but I will take it under serious consideration." Jeremy smiles.

"Maybe it should be G you have the conversation with. Devon didn't come up with this on his own," Ashley smiles back. "Now, I'm going to join Devon." She closes her eyes and dozes off with the smile still on her face.

When Ashley wakes up two hours later, she is wrapped in Jeremy's arms. "Is our visitor gone?" she asks.

Jeremy laughs. "Yeah, I read G the riot act about letting him out of her sight. She claims she does not know about the mama comment, though." Ashley snuggles closer to Jeremy.

"I could lie in your arms forever," she whispers. "I, I didn't mean to say that," Ashley quickly says aloud.

"Say what?" Jeremy asks.

"Nothing, Jeremy."

"Ashley, Sadie called. They found your mother right where your father said she was. Dental records positively identified her. I know you need to take care of her soon. I would be honored if you would let me go with you."

"Jeremy, aren't you tired of taking care of me? It seems like that's all you've done since I got here."

"You know what I'm tired of? Going over two hours without kissing you," Jeremy replies, leaning over Ashley and kissing her deeply. "Ashley, I'm so proud of you. I wish I had your strength and courage to confront my family."

"You will when it's time, Jeremy, and I'll be by your side if you want me to be," Ashley replies, kissing him again several times.

Finally, Jeremy breaks off the kissing. "I bet you're hungry."

"I am. What time is it?"

"Noon."

"Oh, my gosh. I need to get up and check on the workers."

"It's fine, baby girl. They started work early this morning. Since it's Friday, Hank gave them the afternoon off. So you have all weekend."

"I can't do much with my arm in this brace. I think I remember the doctor saying to come back in a week and get a cast. Is that right?" Ashley asks.

"It is. Now, let me help you up." He helps Ashley out of bed. When she says ouch, Jeremy says, "do you need a pain pill?"

"No, they make me goofy."

"I haven't seen you goofy yet. I might like you that way." Ashley pokes him in the ribs and laughs. "I'll help you dress. G went and got you some clothes this morning."

"Let me try myself first," Ashley says. Jeremy nods and leaves the room. When he returns, Ashley is sitting on the bed crying.

"Ashley, what's wrong?"

"I can't fasten my bra."

"Leave it off, then. I won't mind," Jeremy states, grinning.

"I don't think that would be a good idea with my size," Ashley says, wiping her tears away.

"I'll fasten it for you."

"Maybe G could. I don't want you to see my scars."

"Baby girl, I want to see all of you one day when you're ready," Jeremy says, kneeling in front of her. He lifts her chin, so she has to look into his eyes. "You are a beautiful woman inside and out in my eyes." Ashley nods and stands.

As she turns her back to Jeremy, he stands closely behind her. Starting at her shoulders, Jeremy places a tiny kiss on every scar down to the waistband of Ashley's pants. "Soon, I'll finish what I started," he whispers in her ear. "Now, let me try to fasten your bra. I'm used to unfastening it, so it may take me a few seconds to figure it out." Ashley giggles at the comment, so Jeremy deliberately takes longer than necessary to do the job.

Chapter 36

JEREMY

After the pair eats lunch, they and Devon walk to the line shack to view the workers' progress. Ashley retrieves a legal pad and pen from the cabin, and Jeremy writes her instructions for the workers. During lunch, Ashley decided she wanted to take care of her mother's remains on Monday. Since Jeremy is going with her, he offers to fly them to Tennessee on his jet. Ashley will leave the instructions with Hank for the two or three days she is gone.

When Ashley and Jeremy finish, they sit on the porch and watch Devon play with his trucks. "Ashley, can I ask you something? Of course, you don't have to answer if you don't want to." Ashley nods. Jeremy takes her hand in his. "What happened after Sadie took you to the hospital?"

Ashley smiles. "Sadie took me home with her because I had nowhere to go. She and her husband took me in until I graduated from high school. You'll get to meet Al when we get there. They never had kids, so they kind of adopted me, not legally, of course. Sadie made sure I got caught up on all my schoolwork. I graduated at the top of my class and got a scholarship to Arizona State. During my junior year, Wesley was traveling around seeking interns. I interviewed with him. I interned at his firm during the last semester of my senior year. I guess Wesley liked my work because he hired me on graduation day. The rest is history, as they say."

"Thank you for sharing that with me," Jeremy says, squeezing her hand.

"Jeremy, I've learned to trust you with my past, but I have to ask you an earnest question. I want you to answer honestly. I can live with whatever you say. Is there a possibility of a future together that I can trust you with?"

"I've given that some serious thought, Ashley. I hope there is a future for us. I don't want to be with anyone else."

"Papa, mama," Devon yells, running toward the pair.

"You haven't had the talk yet," Ashley says, grinning, the seriousness of their private moment shattered by a little boy.

"No, I've been trying to decide if it's needed," Jeremy says, grabbing and lifting the little boy.

After dinner, Ashley tells Jeremy she wants to sleep at the line shack. She tells him she must sleep alone for a few nights to discover if the nightmares are gone. Besides, it's time for Devon to return to his papa's bedroom. Jeremy grudgingly agrees, but demands extra make out time for his sacrifice. She also asks to borrow his SUV because she needs to go into town the following morning.

The couple leaves early Monday morning for the flight to Tennessee. Jeremy hired a pilot to fly the jet so he could be with Ashley during the flight. Once at the Tennessee hotel, Jeremy surprises Ashley with a two-bedroom suite so she can continue to sleep alone. So far, she hasn't had any nightmares, but Jeremy wants to be nearby if needed.

Jeremy accompanies Ashley to a funeral home to plan for her mother. Next, they visit a cemetery. Ashley picks out a beautiful plot overlooking the Smoky Mountains as her mother's final resting place. Lastly, they travel to the police station to meet Sadie.

Ashley signs the necessary paperwork for her mother's remains to be released to the funeral home. Finally, the pair are escorted to Sadie's office.

"Ashley," Sadie says, greeting her with a warm smile and a tight hug. Sadie shakes Jeremy's hand. "Thank you for stopping by. Before I forget, Al and I want you to join us for dinner. Al insists on cooking, of course," Sadie laughs. "He's better than he used to be," she adds with a wink.

"Sadie," Jeremy says, sitting in front of her desk. "Have any charges been filed against me that I should know?"

"No, Jeremy. Since Ashley's father confessed, the DA said there was no need."

"Jeremy only did what I asked," Ashley says. "If any charges are filed, they should be against me."

"Everything is fine. Now, let me tell you what's happening. Your father is back in Tennessee. Murder and several other charges related to the crime have been filed against him. They set his bond high because the judge agreed with the DA that he might be a flight risk," Sadie says. "With the help of a few of my contacts, your dad's names and pictures are being shown on all the national news channels and social media."

"That's great news," Ashley says.

"It is, and the Jackson police are helping us out by providing their information as a contact. Now, the bad news, Ashley. Ten women have contacted us, and Jackson has been contacted by six. One woman claims her daughter was molested two days before your father was picked up. I won't go into details, but the story sounds legitimate."

"Oh no," Ashley replies in horror. Jeremy puts his arm around her shoulders. "I imagine there are more. It breaks my heart for those people. What will happen?"

"There will be investigations, of course. Some cases may be too old to prosecute, but those people may be called to testify in court if willing. Your father will die in prison, that's for sure."

"I hope so," Ashley says. "He doesn't deserve ever to feel the sun on his face again."

"Ashley, when is the service for your mother?"

Ashley looks at Jeremy, who pulls her closer to him. "We decided on a graveside service tomorrow at 2:00 at Green Hills Cemetery. We found a beautiful spot for her."

"Is there anyone I can contact for you?" Sadie asks.

Ashley shakes her head, but Jeremy speaks up. "I think it would be nice if the people from the church were notified. After all, it sounds like Ashley's mother was a wonderful minister's wife."

Ashley looks at him with tears in her eyes. "Thank you, Jeremy."

Sadie walks around her desk and takes Ashley's free hand. "I can do that. We'll see you for dinner at 7:00. Please come hungry. Al thinks he has to cook for a crowd."

Chapter 37

ASHLEY

The service for her mother was hard for Ashley. Even though she had been grieving the loss of her mother for ten years, the funeral service was so final. It surprised Ashley at how many people from the church attended. Each one made it a point to speak to Ashley and share warm memories of her mother. Jeremy stood beside Ashley the entire time, ensuring she was holding up to the strain.

After the service, Ashley took Jeremy to the house. They walked through the old structure. Ashley felt it was an essential part of her healing process. Finally, she laid a bouquet on a fresh mound of dirt where Ashley knew they had found her mother.

Jeremy ordered dinner from room service, and Ashley took a long, hot bath. After the bath, Ashley opened her suitcase and took out a package. She carefully opened the package, revealing a white silk negligee with matching thong panties. The delicate gown has spaghetti straps with a see-thru lace insert between the built-in bra and the panty line. Ashley slips on the gown, careful not to snag it on the brace. Then, she looks in the full-length mirror. The gown hugs her curves perfectly. Then, Ashley sits on the bed.

I bought this Saturday morning after Jeremy said he didn't want to be with anyone else; she remembers. I believe he will hurt me at some point because I've fallen in love with him. I'm ready to trust him now and see what the future holds for me and us.

Ashley opens her door and sees Jeremy's bedroom door open. She tiptoes to the door. He is sitting at a desk with his laptop. His back is to her. "Jeremy, are you busy?"

He doesn't turn around but answers, "I'm trying to figure out a way to track your brother down. Do you need me?"

"Jeremy, I need you very much right now," Ashley says in a low voice.

Chapter 38

JEREMY

Ashley needs me registers in Jeremy's brain at record speed. Concerned about her well-being, he closes his laptop and then turns around. Standing in the doorway is the most beautiful woman he has ever seen. Ashley looks like a Greek goddess wearing a white negligee. Her skin glows, and her black hair shines. Her smile is timid. Jeremy's heart feels like it is ready to explode in his chest.

"You are gorgeous."

"Thank you," the goddess before him whispers as she appears to float to him.

"Are you sure?" Jeremy asks breathlessly.

"Yes, please. I want you," Ashley says, stopping beside the bed. She bends and pulls the bed covers down. "Now," she whispers.

Jeremy planned to leave early the following morning. So he wasn't surprised when his pilot called at 11:00 to ask about the arrangements. Jeremy told him and the co-pilot to take the day off. He was rescheduling the flight for the next morning.

"Who was that?" Ashley asks, yawning and stretching in the bed beside Jeremy.

"Just the pilot. I instructed him to take the day off. I was busy in bed with you."

Ashley looks appalled. "No, you didn't."

Jeremy tickles her and laughs. "No, baby girl. I just told him to take the day off. I'm sure he can come to his own conclusions about the reason."

"My arm, my arm," Ashley says. Jeremy immediately stops tickling her.

"Sorry, baby girl. I forgot." He rolls over on his back and looks at the ceiling. Ashley quickly climbs on top of him, pinning him down.

"Wait a minute," Jeremy says. "Were you faking the pain?" Ashley giggles and leans down to kiss him.

"What's the plan for today?" she asks.

"We are not leaving this bed except to eat and go to the bathroom." Jeremy places his hands on Ashley's hips.

"What do you have in mind that will take all day?" she whispers.

"This," Jeremy replies, rolling Ashley over on her back.

Jeremy and Ashley board the jet the following morning to head back to Wyoming. After takeoff, Jeremy yawns. "I think I'll take a nap. I haven't gotten much rest over the last two days," he grins at Ashley. "Care to join me? Maybe we could christen the bed."

Ashley rolls her eyes but follows him to the small bedroom. Later, as she naps, Jeremy watches Ashley. What a woman, he thinks. She proved to be a force to be reckoned with in bed for someone that was a virgin. Jeremy had never experienced the feelings and emotions he felt when in bed with Ashley. You loved every minute of it, didn't you, his inner voice asks? I wonder why that is? Because I enjoy her company, Jeremy answers. When will you admit you're in love with Ashley? The voice asks. I'm not, he declares. You are, the voice says. Finally, he drifts off to sleep with his baby girl in his arms.

"We've been cleared for landing," the pilot's voice says over the intercom, waking Jeremy and Ashley. They quickly dress, move to seats in the middle of the plane, and buckle their seatbelts.

"Jeremy, we should probably talk about sleeping arrangements," Ashley says as Jeremy drives to the ranch.

He reaches for her hand and squeezes it. "I was hoping this day would come. I've already made arrangements. Everything is taken care of besides mamas and papas sleep together."

"Does it bother you he calls me that?"

"No, Ashley, it doesn't. I'm delighted Devon loves you as he does. When I take him back to Mike and Michelle's, I need to discuss it with them."

"That's going to be here soon. I've only got two more weeks. I think the project will be finished next week," Jeremy hears a touch of sadness in Ashley's voice.

"I know, baby girl, but don't worry. We'll work something out. I promise."

At the ranch, Jeremy and Hank carry the suitcases to the bedrooms. Devon holds Ashley's hand, practically dragging her behind them.

"Mama, come look at my new big boy bed," Devon says, pulling Ashley into her bedroom. Ashley's queen size bed is gone. In its place is a twin-size bed shaped like a dump truck with safety rails on the sides. Devon jumps on the bed. "Now, you and papa can sleep together all the time.

"That's the idea, little man," Jeremy says, walking up behind Ashley and wrapping his arm around her waist. "I must warn you, though, one of us men is very messy in the bathroom. I'll let you figure out which one," Jeremy whispers in her ear and gently nibbles on her earlobe.

"You're insatiable," Ashley whispers and moans.

"Me? You started it on the plane."

"Let's check on the line shack before the workers leave for the day. My doctor's appointment is early in the morning, so I need to see if they need instructions for tomorrow."

"Maybe they will leave early today, and we can try out the beds in the line shack."

"Really, Jeremy?"

"Yes, I want you on every surface I can find available. If I can't find one, we'll improvise." Jeremy slaps her behind as he backs away. "Devon, let's go to the line shack."

Chapter 39

ASHLEY

Ashley is pleased with the amount of work done while she was gone. She talks to the workers while Jeremy and Devon play in the dirt nearby. Ashley tells the men she will be late tomorrow and gives them a list of items to do until she gets there.

As the workers leave for the day, G walks up and tells Ashley Jarod was there while she was gone. Jarod appeared pleased with the work but wants to talk to Ashley about moving forward on his father's house. Jeremy walks up as the two women finish up their conversation.

"Ashley, I like what you've done to the line shack," G says. " I would love you to make similar changes to my house."

"I would like that very much, G. I'm almost ready to tell the Marshes I quit."

"Why?" Jeremy asks, surprised.

"Because I can't find a suitable place for it. Yes, there's plenty of wide open space to build a house on the ranch. I've grown to love it here and don't want to spoil the pristine beauty," Ashley says, waving her arm across the valley.

"Thank you, Ashley," G says.

"Yeah, thanks, baby girl. I think you appreciate the beauty almost as much as G and I do," Jeremy says. "G, would you take Devon back with you?"

G grins. "Devon, let's see if we can help Hank with dinner." Devon runs up to her, takes her hand, and the two walk toward the house.

"Smooth, Jeremy. Very smooth," Ashley giggles.

"I think G was young once," he replies. He grabs her hand and drags her into the cabin.

Jeremy insists on driving Ashley to her doctor's appointment the following morning. She gets a cast on her arm that she must wear for at least six weeks. Per Ashley's request, Jeremy stops at a pharmacy and waits in the SUV. She soon returns, carrying a small bag.

When the couple walks in the door, Devon spies Ashley's cast. "Want one," he declares.

"Devon, you can't have one like this because your arm's not broken. I can fix you up with something, though. Let's go to your bedroom." Jeremy and G look at each other in confusion.

Ten minutes later, Devon and Ashley return to the living room. Devon has an ace bandage wrapped around his arm, which he shows off proudly. "Mama, take care of me," Devon announces to everyone. After lunch, Devon accompanies Ashley to the line shack to show off his bandaged arm to the workers.

After lunch, there isn't much Ashley can do with her broken arm except get in the way of the workers. So when Jeremy arrives, he, Ashley, and Devon walk down to the valley. While Devon plays in the stream, Ashley and Jeremy watch from a nearby boulder. Ashley remembers G's statement about building Jeremy a home on the ranch. Ashley asks his thoughts about a house, knowing exactly where she will build it.

Jeremy's tastes are simple. He wants views of the mountains and valley. He says he would like a skylight over his bed to watch the storms and the stars. At least one fireplace in the house is a must, he says. Four bedrooms with separate bathrooms for each would be nice for visitors. Jeremy says he has no preference when she asks about one or two stories.

Not wanting to seem too nosy, Ashley tells Jeremy it's time for Devon's nap. They walk back to the house, where all three nap on Jeremy's bed, much to his dismay.

The following two weeks pass by too quickly for Ashley. The work at the line shack is completed, and Ashley begins designing the upgrades to G's house.

Unfortunately, she will only be able to do about one-half of the work on G's house that she did on the line shack because of trees and the mountainside.

Ashley and Jeremy agree to fly out with Devon on Sunday morning. The plan is for Jeremy to drop Ashley at her apartment and then take Devon to Mike and Michelle's. He will spend Sunday night with Ashley and fly back to Wyoming on Monday morning.

Chapter 40

JEREMY

After dinner the night before they are scheduled to leave, Ashley takes a walk alone. She carries a blanket with her. Jeremy watches her leave the house, knowing something is bothering Ashley. He follows at a distance. Ashley lays the blanket down when she reaches her and Jeremy's favorite spot below the line shack. She looks across the valley for a long time. As Jeremy watches, Ashley sits down, pulling her knees up. She rests her chin on her knees. It is so quiet on the mountainside that Jeremy hears Ashley's barely audible sobs.

Jeremy lets her cry for a while and then sits down beside her. "What's bothering you, Ashley?"

"It's nothing. You'll think it's silly."

"No, I won't. Talk to me, please," Jeremy says.

"Oh, Jeremy. I hate to leave this place. I've grown to love everyone here, and it feels like I'm leaving my family," Ashley replies. "See, I told you it was silly. I'm just hormonal right now. It's that time, you know."

"Ashley, you are part of this little family. You aren't leaving permanently. You can come back to visit whenever you want."

"I know, and I appreciate it. I really do."

"But you think things will change, don't you? You think Devon and I will change how we feel about you? That's it, isn't it?" Ashley nods and begins crying again. "Come here." Jeremy takes her in his arms, and they lie on the blanket.

"Devon will be in Vegas during the week. You can see him whenever you want. I'll make sure of it."

Ashley utters a tiny "okay."

Chapter 41

ASHLEY

Jeremy is quieter than usual on the drive to the airport and the flight to Vegas. He flies the plane himself, leaving Ashley to entertain Devon. *I don't mind,* Ashley thinks. *I love this little boy probably more than I should. At least I'll get to see him in Vegas.*

After dropping Ashley off at her apartment, Jeremy leaves to take Devon back to Mike and Michelle's. Expecting Jeremy to return as planned, Ashley makes a quick trip to the food store and prepares dinner for her and Jeremy. However, by 7:00 pm, Jeremy still hasn't shown up. Finally, at 8:00, he calls and says Devon was distraught when Jeremy got ready to leave, so he decided to stay at Mike and Michelle's with Devon. Although she's very disappointed, Ashley says she understands.

Ashley is at the office early Monday morning to meet with Wesley. First, she updates him on the line shack and that G wants her to work on her house. Then, they discuss Jeremy's father's house. Ashley tells Wesley she can't complete the project because she can't find a suitable location for a home that large. She also tells him she doesn't want to do the project and deal with Jarod. Wesley says he understands and will set up a meeting with Jeremy's father.

The rest of the week is spent catching up with Ashley's clients and meetings. However, she went shopping for two new outfits, hoping Jeremy might take her dancing again. Ashley assumed she would spend every weekend at the ranch with

Jeremy, but she hadn't heard from him by Friday morning. Hurt by his action, Ashley throws herself into working on plans for G's house.

By the middle of the following week, there still hasn't been any word from Jeremy. Ashley needs to move forward on G's house and calls her. "G, I need to come this weekend and order supplies and contact workers for the job."

"Great," G replies. "I'll pick you up at the airport."

"No need for that, G. I'll stay in town," Ashley replies.

"Ashley, you can stay here. Jeremy is in Vegas for a couple of weeks."

"Oh," Ashley says.

"I take it he didn't tell you," G pauses when she hears silence on Ashley's end of the phone.

After a few seconds, Ashley says, "okay. I'll stay with you this time."

Ashley flies to Wyoming early Saturday morning. G meets her at the airport. They talk about everything but Jeremy on the way to the ranch. Once they arrive, Ashley surveys the house again and double-checks her supplies list. Finally, she borrows G's car and drives back into town. Ashley ordered supplies and arranges for delivery in two weeks. Next, she contacts each worker she used to see if they will be available to work for her before returning to the ranch at dinnertime.

Ashley lies in Jeremy's bed that night, missing him terribly. As much as she loves spending time with G, the emptiness of Jeremy's absence makes her want to leave earlier. So she grabs her phone and looks up her flight time for Sunday. Ashley planned to leave early evening but now changes it to lunchtime. Ashley cries herself into a restless sleep.

Chapter 42

JEREMY

Ashley's vanilla shampoo and body wash welcome Jeremy to his bedroom Tuesday afternoon when he walks in. So she was here, he thinks, inhaling deeply. Ashley didn't tell me she was coming. No, you idiot, and you didn't tell her you've been in Vegas the past two weeks either, the inner voice says. I know. I know. I needed some time away from her. Things were getting too deep, Jeremy tells the voice. Congratulations. Now she probably has figured out you only used her for the sex, the voice answers. No, it wasn't like that at all, Jeremy replies. Are you sure because you haven't spoken to her since you took her and Devon back to Vegas? Leave me alone, Jeremy says.

Jeremy sits on his bed with his head in his hands. The voice is right. He hasn't called or seen Ashley since that day. He needed a break from her to clear his head. It helped that he spent his days taking photos for the Vegas visitor's bureau's social media advertising. Unfortunately, all Jeremy did at night was miss Ashley in his arms. I'll see her Friday night, he decides. Then we can spend all weekend together.

On Wednesday, Jeremy spends the day constructing a makeshift photo-developing studio. He had all the supplies since he temporarily closed his studio in Mexico and shipped everything to the ranch. Jeremy worked late into the night, Wednesday reviewing the photos on his computer and selecting his favorites. On Thursday, he developed his favorites into photographs for his meeting with the visitor's bureau on Tuesday in Vegas.

Jeremy packs his bag and places the photographs into a box on Friday. He kisses G goodbye and is flying to Vegas by 4:00 pm. He didn't call Ashley because he plans to surprise her. The thought of seeing her again makes his heart beat faster.

Chapter 43

ASHLEY

Although not a social person, Ashley is looking forward to the cocktail party tonight. It is being held in her honor by the hotel's owner because her work is completed. The hotel will open to the public in two months. This party will give me a chance to wear one of my new dresses. Ashley does her hair and makeup and puts on the navy cocktail dress. It isn't nearly as expensive as the red one Jeremy bought her, but looks just as good. The dress is very short with a V-neckline. The pushup bra Ashley bought adds a little extra cleavage. She smiles as she looks in the mirror. Ashley gathers her white wrap and clutch. She walks into her living room carefully, not used to wearing five-inch heels.

When there's a knock on the door, Ashley expects it to be the limo driver that is picking her up. But instead, Jeremy is standing at the door, looking down at a box in his hands. He walks in and dumps the box on her dining room table.

"Hi, Ashley. I thought you could help me pick up photos for the visitor's bureau's media advertising campaign."

"Jeremy, you can't barge in here unexpectedly," Ashley says, closing the door. He finally looks at her, and there is a stunned look on his face. "You should have called first."

"Ah, you're going out?" he murmurs.

"Yes, I am." Then there's another knock on the door. "That should be my driver," Ashley says, opening the door to find the limo driver dressed in a black suit. "Go get Devon to help you with the pictures and lock the door on your way out," Ashley spews angrily as she slams it behind her.

Ashley fumes all the way to the party. How dare Jeremy just show up after three weeks she thinks? He just assumed it would thrill me to see and welcome him with open arms. He believed I would be just sitting around waiting for him to appear. Well, now I am twice as glad I'm attending the party.

The party is lovely, and Ashley enjoys it very much. Several people ask about the sustainable features she incorporated into the design. Ashley gives them a quick tour. She's surprised when she looks at her watch, noticing four hours have passed. Ashley instructs the driver to take her to a casino nearby as she gets into the limo. She tells him she will get a ride back to her apartment later.

Not wanting to take a chance on Jeremy still being at her apartment, Ashley spends two hours learning the game of five-card stud. She loses at first but ends up walking out of the casino with an additional $500 in her purse. In addition, Ashley has the phone numbers of two very attractive men from the poker table. Ashley smiles, remembering how the men flirted with her as she climbs into the cab for the ride home.

Ashley unlocked the door quietly. The living room lights are on, and Jeremy is asleep on her sofa. Ashley rolls her eyes and contemplates waking him. Instead, she retrieves a blanket from her bedroom and covers him. Next, Ashley walks into her bedroom and locks the door. Finally, she undresses, washes her face, and climbs into bed. Although her body aches for Jeremy's touch, Ashley refuses to give in and go to him. After a while, she falls asleep, dreaming of the many nights she spent in Jeremy's bed.

The following morning, Ashley wakes with the sunrise. She climbs out of bed and quietly opens her bedroom door. Jeremy and the box of photos are gone. The blanket is neatly folded on the sofa. A piece of paper lies on top. Ashley walks over and picks up the paper. It is a note from Jeremy apologizing for his behavior and saying he hoped she had a good time. That's it. No, I'll see you soon, or I miss you, nothing. You've been used, Ashley's inner voice tells her. He used her as a babysitter for Devon and sex. It's time to move on. I know, but she replies, but I've landed in love with him. The voice says he doesn't feel the same way.

Chapter 44

JEREMY

"I am so stupid," Jeremy says aloud, driving to a hotel. "I assumed Ashley would be happy to see me." The inner voice says you expected her to be sitting at home waiting for you. Didn't you? You are such a fool. You don't have to remind me, Jeremy answers. What are you going to do, the voice asks? I do not know, Jeremy answers.

After checking into the hotel, Jeremy dumps the photos on the floor. He sits down next to them and starts to go through each one, but he can't concentrate. Finally, Jeremy tosses the images in his hand to the floor and leans his back against the sofa. He closes his eyes, remembering Ashley last night. She looked beautiful in that short navy dress. It would have highlighted her blue eyes if they hadn't been so full of anger. The V neckline was lower than usual, showing off Ashley's cleavage, which was screaming "touch me" to Jeremy.

I need to get away. I think I'll go to Mexico for a few weeks and surf. Maybe that will clear my mind. I'll talk to Devon about it this afternoon. I'll try to leave next weekend.

Monday morning, Jeremy gets a phone call from Wesley. A meeting between Jeremy's father, brother, G, Ashley and Wesley has been set up for Thursday in Wesly's conference room. Jeremy is welcome to join if he so chooses. Jeremy says he will think about it.

Chapter 45

ASHLEY

Ashley has spent all week preparing for this morning's meeting. She knows the Marsh father and son will not be happy with her decision. Wesley told Ashley in a meeting yesterday that he backed her one hundred percent and would take the brunt of their ire. Ashley dresses in a black suit with a white blouse. The skirt conservatively touches the top of her knees. She pulls her hair back into a bun before putting on her three-inch heels. Ashley looks in the mirror, pleased with her chosen battle fatigues.

Three minutes before the start of the meeting, Ashley enters the conference room, surprised to see Jeremy and G also in attendance. She takes the only available seat, which is between Wesley and Jeremy. G greets Ashley with a warm hello, but Jeremy ignores her.

"Well, shall we get started?" Wesley asks. Everyone nods, and he turns toward Ashley.

Before she can begin, Jarod speaks up, looking at G and Jeremy. "If we had known the two of you were coming, we would have sent the jet for you."

"No, need for that," Jeremy says. "We came in mine."

"You have a jet?" Jeremy's father asks.

"Yes, and it even has a bed," Jeremy replies sarcastically. Ashley looks at Wesley, and he shrugs his shoulders.

"I suppose you bought it on clearance and will make payments on it for the rest of your life," Jarod says snidely.

"Actually, it was brand new, and I paid cash for it."

Jarod sits back in his seat with a smug look on his face. "I never thought my brother would be a drug runner."

"I think we should get back to the purpose of this meeting," Wesley says. "You, Marshes, can finish this conversation later."

"Sorry, Wesley, but this is happening now. I'm tired of this crap," Jeremy replies.

G reaches over and pats him on the arm. "Do you really want to do this now?" she whispers. Jeremy nods.

"I'm not a drug runner and never have been. All the money I have has been the fruit of my labor. After I quit college and didn't receive a penny from you, father, G did loan me the money to get started."

"And what exactly do you do?" Jeremy's father asks. Ashley watches the exchange with curiosity. This could be Jeremy's showdown with his family, she thinks.

"I am a highly respected photographer. I have clients all over the world. They have published my photos in the most prestigious magazines," Jeremy says.

"Really?" Jarod says. "I've never seen your pictures."

"That's because you don't read those types of magazines. You know, the ones with landscapes and wildlife. If you had a life outside architecture and high-priced whores, you might have seen one in a doctor's office."

"Jeremy, that's enough," his father says.

"Old man, I'm sick and tired of you and Jarod constantly looking down on me and my lifestyle. You do not know what I do or where I even live. So I will say one last thing and then shut up. Perhaps you should look up at me instead of down at me. After all, I'm number forty-eight on the list for the top fifty richest men in America under forty," Jeremy says.

Ashley watches as Jeremy's father's and brother's jaws drop. She touches Jeremy's arm and whispers, "I'm proud of you." He doesn't look at her, but nods his thanks.

"Okay, I think we should take a quick break and then get into the reason for our meeting," Wesley says, standing. "There's coffee and pastries on the credenza."

Ashley exits the room and goes down the hall to the restroom. G follows her. "Ashley, my dear. Thank you."

"For what, G. I haven't done anything."

"You don't know it, but you gave Jeremy the courage to confront his family. He watched what you did to your father. I guess he decided it was his turn. Now, perhaps, he can move on with his life."

"I hope so," Ashley says as she turns, walking out of the room. She doesn't want to get into a conversation about her and Jeremy's relationship, or lack of it, these days.

As Ashley walks into the conference room, she remains standing, prepared to show her presentation to the group. She waits while the others take their seats. Each has a cup of coffee in their hands except Jeremy, who holds a glass of bourbon.

When everyone is finally seated, and Ashley is ready, it is G who speaks first. "I must say I'm disappointed you didn't speak to me about a house being built on my ranch," she says, staring across the table at Jeremy's father and brother. "Second, there is no way I'm leaving the ranch to you when I die. From now on, you are not welcome there as long as I live." G reaches into her purse and pulls out two checks. She shoves one across the table to Jeremy's father. "Here's a blank check to reimburse you for any supplies Ashley purchased while working on your project and any other expenditures she may have charged to your credit card." The next one is pushed toward Wesley. "Wesley, this pays for Ashley's time working on the project. The remaining money goes toward her retainer for my project. This meeting is over," G states, rising from her chair.

Jeremy also stands. "One more thing before we go. Jarod, that so-called brat at the ranch Ashley said was her son, is actually my son. So now, G and I will concentrate the rest of the day taking MY son to the park." Jeremy takes G's arm, and they leave the room.

Ashley watches in awe as Jeremy and G leave. G saved her from the Marshes' wrath and validated her work. She watches as the two remaining Marsh men leave the room without saying a word to her or Wesley. She drops into her chair and looks at Wesley.

"Well, I have to say that was the most entertaining meeting I've ever been in," Wesley says with a grin. "I'm glad Jeremy finally got things off his chest. He's been carrying that weight around for years. Ashley, it appears we have a new client. Apparently, the workers you hired have been talking in town because I've had so many calls. I think opening a branch office in Jackson will happen sooner than I thought. Next time you go, I want you to look at office space. Of course, the branch office is yours if you want it."

"Oh wow. Thanks, Wesley, but I don't know anything about running an office."

"We'll hire an expert office manager to help you so you can focus on designing and building."

"Can I think about it?" Ashley asks.

"Sure thing, Ashley. Let's start with the office space first. I think we will need at least enough space for four architects." Ashley nods. "Let's go out to lunch to celebrate."

Ashley is busy with meeting all afternoon, so she doesn't have time to reflect on the meeting until she returns home late in the evening. I'm so proud Jeremy confronted his family, she thinks. I hope he feels better. And he admitted that Devon is his son. G sure shocked everyone as well, including me. So now it looks like I have some decisions to make.

Chapter 46

JEREMY

"Man, that felt good," Jeremy tells G as they exit the building.

"It did. I'm proud of you, Jeremy."

"You sure surprised everyone, too, G."

"Well, it was time I had my say. Let's grab some lunch and change clothes before we pick up Devon. I really don't care for sand in my suit and heels," she laughs.

Devon sits down in a pile of sand with his trucks. While Jeremy and G listen to little boy truck sounds, they sit on a nearby picnic bench.

"G, I'm leaving on Saturday to go to Mexico. I want to get some surfing in before ski season, and I miss my friends."

"You miss the partying and the girls," G says, watching him out of the corner of her eye.

"I guess I miss that too," he replies, deep in thought.

"What about Ashley? I thought the two of you were moving past the friendship stage."

"It was always friendship. If she thought there was more, she was mistaken. I know she cares about Devon. I talked to Mike and Michelle. Ashley can see him whenever she wants," Jeremy says.

"Have you talked to her? About the friendship, I mean."

"No, I thought it best to let things die down."

G looks at him. "Jeremy, look at me." He does. "Exactly who was it best for?" she asks, standing and going over to play with Devon.

It was best for me, Jeremy thinks. That's the way it is with women. You have a good time, and then you move on. That way, there are no ties and no future expectations. That's the way it will always be for me.

Jeremy's jet lands a little before 9:00 pm in Oaxaca, Mexico. Jeremy drops his luggage off at his condo, then heads to his favorite bar. Many of his friends are there and spend the entire night drinking and dancing. Jeremy's female friends and local women are plentiful. After several drinks, he spies a woman in a short red dress and black hair. He walks over to her, intending to ask her to dance to a slow song. However, when the woman turns around, it is not Ashley. Jeremy quickly backs away, returning to his table, disappointed.

At noon the following day, Jeremy wakes to find himself tangled up with an unknown female in what he assumes is her bed. He jumps up, runs to the bathroom, and throws up. As he stands, the woman appears and tries to pull him back to the bed. Jeremy refuses and quickly dresses. Unfortunately, he doesn't remember where his car is and has to call a friend for a ride to his condo. Instead of the condo, the friend returns Jeremy to the bar to retrieve his car.

Once at the condo, Jeremy is disgusted with himself. As he showers, Jeremy vows that his night with a strange woman won't happen again. Sunrise and sunset times are spent showing off Jeremy's surfing prowess. Women gather on the beach to watch and marvel at his maneuvers on a surfboard and boogie board. Nights are spent in bars and in bed with a different woman every night. Afternoons are spent sleeping and dreaming of the woman he left in Vegas.

After three months and four visits to a doctor for an STD, Jeremy decides to return to Wyoming to prepare for the skiing season. Thankfully, none of the STDs are permanent.

$$Chapter\ 47$$

ASHLEY

Ashley spends her next three months off and on in Wyoming working on G's house. However, she refuses to spend her nights on the ranch, so she stays at an extended-stay hotel and makes the forty-five-minute drive twice a day. She flies commercially home every other weekend and returns with Devon several times. G told Ashley that Jeremy was in Mexico, but Ashley never inquires about him or if he is in contact with Devon.

The workers Ashley hired are the same ones from before. They rarely need instructions because much of the work is the same, only on a larger scale. This allows Ashley the time she needs to look for office space. Finally, during the third month of G's project, Ashley finds the space in Jackson to accommodate Wesley's wishes. First, however, it will need remodeling.

Wesley flies to Jackson and is pleased with space. It is a free-standing building with a large apartment above it that needs updating. Although Ashley hasn't decided whether to move to Jackson, she agrees to design the office space and apartment. Wesley tells Ashley she can live in the apartment if she chooses to run the branch office.

Ashley knows Thanksgiving is two weeks away. G's home project will be completed in two days. So Ashley returns to Vegas and works on the office building design. Ski season will start then, and Jeremy will return home. Ashley does not want to be in Jackson when he returns, but her work demands it.

She turns down G's invitation to Thanksgiving dinner, choosing to remain alone in her hotel room. A knock on the door interrupts Ashley's concentration on Thanksgiving morning. She opens the door, and Devon jumps into her arms.

"Mama, come with us to watch papa ski."

"I don't think I can, sweetheart. I have a lot of work to do," Ashley replies as G enters the room.

"Come with us, Ashley. Jeremy is doing the inaugural run down the new ski slope today. We will watch from the lodge's balcony," G says.

"Please, mama. Please." Ashley looks into the little boy's pleading eyes and can't refuse.

"Okay, Devon. Let me get dressed. I'll go, but I'm taking my car so I can leave afterward."

Two hours later, G, Devon and Ashley stand at the center of the balcony waiting for Jeremy to make the run. Ashley has never skied and is shocked at the crowd gathered below them. Ashley lifts Devon and places him on the railing so he can see better. She holds him tightly, so he doesn't slip off.

Finally, music begins playing loudly. The crowd erupts into cheering and yelling Jeremy's name. Jeremy waves to the crowd from the top of the lift and then nods at a man standing beside him.

Ashley holds her breath as she watches Jeremy begin his descent down the slope. His beautiful dark brown hair flies in the wind. Ashley can't see his face, but she knows Jeremy is smiling. When he reaches the bottom of the slope, he leans forward and tucks the poles closely at his sides. Jeremy flies through the air like a bird. A free bird, just like his spirit, she thinks as her heart swells with pride.

Cheers from the crowd erupt again when Jeremy lands on his feet. He waves to the crowd and skis to a roped-off area, blocking the crowd off. Jeremy pulls off his skis and then carries them and the poles to an opening in the rope. Photographers take his picture as Jeremy removes his helmet. Ashley's breath catches in her throat, and her heart beats faster seeing the man she loves for the first time in months. He drops the skis and poles into the snow before moving through the gap in the rope.

Several people greet Jeremy with slaps on the back and handshakes as he walks through the crowd. Women quickly surround Jeremy, vying for his attention.

Meanwhile, G, Devon and Ashley make their way to the lodge's deck. Before Ashley can catch Devon, he jerks out of her hand and runs toward his papa. The crowd parts for the little boy, who leaps into his father's arms. Jeremy hugs Devon tightly and looks up straight into Ashley's eyes.

Ashley drops her eyes and looks for an escape route, but the crowd is too thick. So instead, she watches as Jeremy carries Devon toward where Ashley and G stand. Jeremy stops in front of Ashley and sets Devon down. Then, placing one hand on her hip and the other behind her neck, Jeremy pulls Ashley to him and kisses her. It's not kiss #1 or kiss #2, but kiss #3 that he places on her lips.

Shocked, Ashley opens her mouth in a gasp. Jeremy takes that as an invitation to enter her mouth. Ashley places her hands on his chest to push him away, but Jeremy refuses to let her go and end the kiss. When he finally does, he looks into her eyes and says, "I love you, baby girl."

Ashley uses more force to push Jeremy away and succeeds. She turns and walks away, refusing to look back when Jeremy and Devon call her name. As soon as she can, Ashley runs to her car and leaves with tears flowing down her cheeks.

With the importance of opening the new slope, Ashley knows Jeremy will be occupied for a while. But it's only a matter of time before someone knocks on her door. Ashley goes to the hotel, packs everything and checks out. Then, she does something she's never done before. She drives to a nightclub close to the airport.

Ashley walks in and heads directly to the bar. She orders a bourbon and thinks while waiting for a drink. Someone sits beside her, and Ashley looks up at Tyler.

"Hi, Ashley. You don't look too good. Let me guess. It has something to do with Jeremy. I heard he's back," Tyler says.

"Tyler, I really don't feel like talking now. You're welcome to sit beside me, but please don't expect me to talk," Ashley says. Tyler nods and sips his drink. After her drink arrives, Ashley takes her phone out of her pocket and turns it on silent. Next, she pulls up flights out of Jackson. Asley sees there's one in an hour to Seattle and books it. Finally, she finishes her drink, which Tyler pays for, and heads to the airport.

Ashley turns in the rental car, checks her bag, and goes through security. At least at this point, no one can bother her. Finally, her flight is called, and Ashley boards her plane, vowing not to return to Jackson.

Chapter 48

JEREMY

J eremy walks to the line shack and sits on the bed he and Ashley shared many times. The door opens slowly. Jeremy looks up, hoping it's Ashley.

"Oh, it's you. I heard you were back," Tyler says.

"Who told you I was back?" Jeremy asks.

"Ashley. Well, she didn't come right out and say it, but seeing how upset she was, I figured it out for myself," Tyler says with a smirk.

Jeremy jumps up. "Ashley? When did you see her and where?"

"I saw her this afternoon at Wylie's bar."

"Wylie's bar? Ashley never goes to a bar," Jeremy says.

"Well, she did today," Tyler replies, enjoying making Jeremy angry.

"Did she say where she was going?"

"No, we walked out together, and I walked her to her car. I didn't see which way she went when she left." Tyler watches Jeremy closely. "Everything alright between you?" Jeremy gives Tyler a mean look and walks past him out the door.

"Well, you didn't get the reception you hoped for, did you, Jeremy?" G asks when he walks into the living room.

"No, and now she's gone," Jeremy says, looking heartbroken.

"What do you mean, gone?"

"I went to the hotel hoping to talk to her, but they said she checked out. I just saw Tyler. He saw her in Wylie's bar this afternoon. Tyler walked her to her car but didn't see which direction she went."

"G, I have no idea. I've called and left several messages. I sent several texts. Ashley hasn't answered any of them."

"Sit down here by me. I've kept my mouth shut long enough, waiting for you to do the right thing. So now, you are going to listen and keep your mouth shut. Do you understand?"

"Yes, ma'am," Jeremy replies, sitting down.

"You hurt her, Jeremy. You did the one thing you said you wouldn't do. She gave herself to you after you led her on. Then you ignored her. Next, you went off to Mexico. Please tell me you didn't bring a permanent health issue back home."

"I didn't," Jeremy says, embarrassed.

"Thank God for that!" G pauses. "I don't know what you are going to do, nor do I have any advice. But, if you do really love her, grow up, be a man, and find a way to earn her trust again. Now, I'm going to bed." G stands and walks out of the room.

Jeremy lies awake all night trying to develop a plan to regain Ashley's trust. But he does not know where she is even to begin trying. Early the following day, Jeremy calls Wesley, asking him to go by Ashley's apartment. An hour later, Wesley calls back and says she's not there. Well, I'm going skiing. The fresh air may help clear my mind so I can plan.

Once the ski lift drops Jeremy off near the new slope, he feels a tiny bit better, taking deep breaths of the cold, fresh air. The line is long, but several people recognize him and let him cut in front of them. When it's his turn, Jeremy steps onto the slope, takes a deep breath and begins his descent. Midway down, he drops one of his poles. Well, that's fine, he thinks. I can still make it. Finally, Jeremy reaches the end of the slope and takes off into the air. He assumes his position and floats through the air. But as he lands, Jeremy's skis get tangled, and he tumbles all the way to the bottom of the hill.

Chapter 49

ASHLEY

It's late Thanksgiving night when Ashley's plane lands in Seattle. She takes a cab to a hotel, strips, and climbs into bed, mentally exhausted. But she can't sleep. Jeremy's kiss and his words constantly run through her mind. If only he had told her he loved her when he took her back to Vegas months ago. Ashley gets out of bed and turns her phone on to set the alarm. She turned the phone off after she got on the plane. Jeremy blew her phone up with calls, voicemails, and texts. None of which she answered, listened to, or read. The phone lights up with notifications. Ashley changes her mind about setting the alarm. She turns the phone off again. Finally, exhaustion takes over, and she sleeps.

The sun is high in the sky when Ashley wakes. The clock beside the bed says 11:00 am. She showers and dresses, then heads downstairs to walk along the pier and clear her mind. As she walks, Ashley touches her lips, remembering Jeremy's kiss. It made her body ache for his touch, which she thought she had finally gotten past missing so much. As she walks, Ashley decides to call Wesley Monday morning. She will tell him she can't work or live in Jackson. Instead, she will complete the design from her Vegas office, but he will have to find another architect to manage it once it opens.

Ashley looks up at the sky when the first raindrop hits the top of her head. She was so lost in her thoughts Ashley didn't notice the sky had clouded over. She looks around and doesn't have any idea where she is. Ashley ducks under the awning of a food truck and asks the truck operator where she is. It turns out that Ashley is almost ten miles from her hotel. She turns her phone on and calls for a cab using the address the food truck's operator gives her.

While waiting for the cab, Ashley looks at the most recent notifications and finds a voicemail from G that was left five hours earlier. G has never interfered or expressed an opinion about the situation between Jeremy and herself, so the phone call is unusual. Concerned there might be a problem with the remodel of the house, Ashley listens to the voicemail.

"Ashley," G's voice says, crying. "Jeremy has been in a terrible accident. He's in intensive care in a coma. Please call me back. I can send the jet for you if you want to come."

Shocked by the message, Ashley steps from under the awning and lets the rain pour down on her. "Oh, God! What should I do?" Ashley screams at the top of her lungs, looking up at the heavens.

The food truck operator pulls Ashley back under the awning out of the rain. "Lady, follow your heart," the operator says as the cab pulls up.

"Thank you," Ashley whispers. She runs to the cab and gives her hotel's address.

Back inside the warmth of her hotel room, Ashley dries off and changes into a warm cotton robe the hotel provides. She sits on the sofa and dials G's number.

"Ashley, thank goodness you finally called back. I was getting worried about you."

"G, what happened?" G explains about the skiing accident. She tells Ashley that Jeremy's brain has swollen. The doctors are watching it closely to see if they need to go in and release some of the pressure. Jeremy has internal injuries, and his legs are broken in several places. Surgery will need to be done on them later. "Ashley, do you want to come? I'll understand if you don't." G says.

"Yes, G. Please send the jet to get me. I'm in Seattle."

"Okay, Ashley. It will be sometime tomorrow. Right now, the jet is on its way to pick up Michelle so she can take Devon back to Vegas. I'll call you as soon as possible with a time and airport."

"Is Devon okay?" Ashley asks.

"I haven't told him about Jeremy. Michelle thinks it is time for him to return to Mike and Michelle's for a while. The doctor's coming in. I'll call you later." G hangs up.

Ashley stares at the phone in her hand for a long time, praying Jeremy will be okay. She's read about head injuries and knows the next twenty-four to forty-eight hours are critical. Ashley also knows the possibility of permanent damage or memory loss is great for head injuries. All she can do is wait for G to call her back and hope for the best. Ashley walks to the window and stares out at the pouring rain. Finally, she calls room service and orders a bottle of bourbon.

Chapter 50

ASHLEY

The two glasses of bourbon didn't help Ashley relax or sleep, so she was awake when G texted her. The jet would arrive at 7:00 am at a private airport outside Seattle. Ashley packed everything and called a cab at 5:30.

At 6:30, Ashley stood on the tarmac with her luggage, waiting for the jet. She shivered in the cold as snowflakes began to fall. Then, finally, after watching the sky for twenty-five minutes, Ashley saw the jet circling the runway and touch down. As the plane approached her, she hoped all this was a dream. The jet would pull up, and Jeremy would be in the cockpit. But tears filled her eyes when she saw a somber Bill there.

The door to the jet opens, and Bill and an unfamiliar man climb down the steps. Bill rushes to Ashley and hugs her tightly as she begins to sob. Ashley barely notices the other man loading her luggage onto the plane.

When her sobbing stops, Bill says, "let's get you on the plane and out of this cold." Ashley nods and lets him lead her onto the jet. When she's seated, Bill asks, "Ashley, when's the last time you ate?"

"I dunno. Two, three days. I don't remember."

"It will take a few minutes to file a flight plan and refuel. I'm going to the terminal and get you something to eat." Ashley nods, and Bill leaves the plane only to stop to talk to the other man.

Bill returns several minutes later with a large cup of coffee and to go plate. He sets the plate in front of Ashley and opens it. Ashley just stares at it.

"Ashley, you need to eat. Jeremy is in excellent hands. The doctors are very experienced with these types of accidents. You need your strength." Ashley nods, continuing to stare down at the plate. Finally, she picks up the plastic fork, but her hand shakes too much to pick up any food. Bill sits beside her and feeds Ashley slowly, as if she were a child. When Ashley can eat no more, she shakes her head at Bill.

The other man boards the jet. Bill leaves his seat to speak to the man for a few minutes and then returns to Ashley. Bill returns, sitting beside Ashley. He buckles her seatbelt. "Ashley, after the jet takes off, I want you to lie down and nap. Okay?" Ashley nods. Minutes later, the jet is in the air. Bill leads her to the small bedroom and closes the door as he leaves. Ashley lies on the bed and falls fast asleep.

After the plane lands, Bill drives Ashley to the hospital. Next, he escorts her to the waiting room, where several people are sitting around talking. Ashley speaks to Jeremy's father and Jarod. Then she is introduced to Jeremy's mother, Jarod's wife, Jeremy's sister, and her husband. Hank and Ida are also there.

"Hank, will you take me to see Jarod?" Ashley asks.

"Of course." As they walk down the hall, Hank says, "Ashley, have you ever been in an intensive care ward?" Ashley replies, no. "It's very intimidating. They hooked Jeremy up to tubes and wires. He looks bad, but he's not in any pain." Ashley sees G slumped over in a chair beside Jeremy's bed when she and Hank reach the glass window. "She refused to leave his side until you got here," Hank says.

"Okay. Well, I'm here now." Ashley says. Hank taps on the window, and G turns around. She sees Ashley and quickly leaves Jeremy's beside. The two women hug tightly and cry.

"Ashley, only one person is allowed in at a time. So you go in and stay as long as you like. Don't let Jeremy's family bully you, either," G says. "Now that you're here, I think I'll get a hotel room here in town and rest for a while. I'll be back later."

Ashley opens the door and walks into the small room. She gasps at the sight of Jeremy lying in bed. So surrounded by machines and hooked up to monitors and a ventilator, he looks so small. Ashley sits beside the bed, picks up his hand, and kisses it. Then the tears flow again, refusing to stop until no more tears are left.

Two days go by at a snail's pace. Jeremy's family and Ashley take turns sitting with him day and night. Occasionally, Jeremy's eyelids flutter slightly, or his fingers move, getting the group's hopes up, but the doctors tell them that's normal. Finally, on day two, the doctors inform the group that the brain swelling is going down. But he warns them Jeremy is still in critical condition.

On day four, Jeremy's brain has returned to its normal size. The ventilator is removed, and he breathes on his own but remains in a coma. Jeremy has no changes on days five, six, or seven. By this time, the family has developed a daily schedule of staying with Jeremy, but Ashley insists on staying with him all night. She reads and talks to him, watches TV, works, and plays games on her phone, all while holding his hand.

Ashley yawns and sets her work aside, and looks at her watch. It reads 3:00 am. Her eyes are tired, so she closes her eyes. Ashley lays her head down next to Jeremy's hand. She feels a tickle in her hair. Ashley reaches up to smooth her hair but feels fingers in it. She doesn't think anything about it because it sometimes happens with Jeremy. Then Ashley hears a very faint "baby girl." She jerks her head up and sees Jeremy looking at her.

"Jeremy, you're awake," Ashley whispers. She pushes the call button for the nurse. The nurse immediately rushes in and begins checking Jeremy. When the nurse asks how he feels, he replies he is exhausted and wants to sleep. The nurse tells him to rest.

Ashley starts to slide her chair away from the bedside, but Jeremy places his hand on hers and says, "please don't leave me." Ashley nods as he closes his eyes and sleeps.

Chapter 51

JEREMY

Jeremy opens his eyes and looks at the woman he loves. She is asleep, sitting in a chair beside his bed with her head in his open palm. Ashley looks exhausted, he thinks. There are dark circles under her eyes, and she's lost weight. He reaches to touch her face with his other hand but can't move it. He can't move his legs, either. "Oh my God, I'm paralyzed, he thinks.

Ashley opens her eyes and smiles at Jeremy. "Good morning, sleepyhead."

"Ashley, am I paralyzed?" he asks if a slow voice.

"Oh no, they tied you down because sometimes when people come out of comas, they react wildly. The doctors didn't want you pulling out your IV or anything."

"Thank God. How long have I been here?" Ashley notices Jeremy's speech is slow.

"Eight days. Oh, Jeremy, I was so scared. Everyone was. Everyone will be by later to see you."

"Everyone?"

"G, Hank and Ida, of course. But your parents, brother, sister and their spouses are also here."

"They are all here for me?"

Ashley smiles. "Yes, just for you. They were all here when I got here. Do you remember what happened?"

"Yes, I was skiing down the slope, flying through the air, and my skis got tangled. I was trying to get them separated. That's all I remember."

"Jeremy, you are such an exceptional skier. How did your skis get tangled?"

"Honestly, my mind was on you and how much I love you," Jeremy replies as four doctors enter the room. Ashley is asked to leave while they examine Jeremy, so she quickly gathers her things and leaves.

The doctors untied Jeremy, poked, prodded, and questioned for the next hour. As he listens, they tell him about the coma, internal injuries, and that his legs are broken and require surgery in a day or two. When he asks how bad his legs are, the doctors reply they will know more after surgery.

After the doctors leave, Jeremy's family members, Hank, and Ida, are allowed to visit, but only for no longer than three minutes each. G is the last one to see Jeremy. As she leaves, Jeremy asks for Ashley and is told she went to the hotel to nap for a while. Jeremy closes his eyes and dozes off, exhausted from all his visitors.

Ashley sits beside the bed when Jeremy wakes from his nap, drawing on a legal pad. "What are you working on?" he asks, making her jump in surprise.

"Hi, Jeremy. How do you feel?"

"Much better since I can move around a little," Jeremy answers, talking slowly.

"Great. Wesley gave me a project to work on here in Jackson. I'm trying to finish it so I can send him the plans."

"Is it a new house or a remodel?

Ashley continues working and says, "it's a remodel of an office building. Wesley wants to open a branch office here. Word about my work has spread, and he's been getting inquiries."

"Will you move to the office here?"

"Jeremy, I haven't decided what I'm going to do," Ashley replies, looking into his eyes.

"Does my telling you I love you influence you?" Before Ashley can answer, two doctors walk in. They inform Jeremy he's scheduled for surgery early tomorrow morning. They also say they expect the surgery to last six hours, but it could be longer depending on the damage. The good news is Jeremy's internal injuries are healing well, but he needs to stay in intensive care for several more days.

Ashley tells the doctors she will pass the information on to everyone. Jeremy's father taps on the window, letting Ashley know he wants to see his son. She puts her things into her tote and tells Jeremy she will see him later, leaving so his dad can enter the room.

Chapter 52

ASHLEY

Everyone arrives early the following day, hoping to see Jeremy before his surgery. But Jeremy only wants to see Ashley. "You didn't answer my question yesterday," he says.

"Honestly, Jeremy, I don't know how to answer it right now. I don't want to think about it. I want you to go into surgery with a clear mind. Okay?" Jeremy nods as hospital staff enters the room to take him to surgery.

Everyone settles in the waiting room. A nurse comes in requesting a phone number so staff can text updates. It will be that person's responsibility to let everyone else phone. Ashley is shocked when Jarod volunteers.

An hour later, Wesley walks into the waiting room. "Wesley," Ashley says, jumping up to hug him. "Thanks for coming."

Surprised by the hug, Wesley blushes and says, "well, I need to check on my old friend, don't I? Plus, you need something to keep yourself busy during the surgery. Grab your plans and discuss them at the office building."

Entering the office building, Ashley pulls out her plans and begins reviewing them with Wesley. Two hours later, she receives a text that the surgery is going well. The two decide to go to brunch before heading back to the hospital.

"Ashley, have you decided about moving here and running the office?" Wesley asks after the two place their food orders.

"I planned to call you Monday a week ago and tell you absolutely not. Now, with Jeremy's accident, I don't know. He may need help after surgery. So please, Wesley, don't wait on me. If you have someone else in mind, proceed with your plans," Ashley tells him. "I can still travel between here and Vegas as needed."

"Hmmm. I wanted you to accept the offer because of your experience and expertise, not because of Jeremy. People are asking for you. Why don't we wait a couple of weeks and see how things go? But, while I'm here, I will find a contractor and start the building. Your plans are excellent, Ashley."

The two return to the hospital waiting room just as a doctor walks in. "I came to tell you that the damage to Jeremy's legs is more extensive than the x-rays showed. I expect the surgery to last at least six to eight more hours. So you may want to leave and get some rest. We'll keep you posted."

Ashley and Jarod decide to stay while everyone else rests at the hotel. Wesley leaves to find a contractor to work on the office building. It appears Jeremy's confrontation with Jarod, Jeremy's accident, or a combination of the two, has softened Jarod's demeanor. First, he and Ashley talk about the work she did at G's house and then about possibilities for his house in Los Angeles.

Everyone reassembles in the waiting room at 6:00 pm. Ashley dozes in her chair while the others remain steadfastly quiet, hoping for news soon. Finally, at 8:00, after twelve hours of surgery, two very exhausted doctors walk into the waiting room.

"They have taken Jeremy to recovery. He should wake up in a few hours and return to intensive care. I know all of you want to see him, and he'll probably ask how the surgery went. I need all of you to be positive because the news isn't good," the older doctor of the two says.

The younger doctor speaks next. "Let's start with good news. I know all of you have been concerned about Jeremy's slow speech. That will improve as his brain heals. There is no sign of permanent brain damage." The doctor pauses and takes a deep breath before continuing. "The bad news is that there's extensive damage to Jeremy's legs. He can no longer do the physical activities he loves, such as skiing, surfing, mountain climbing, etc. We repaired his legs to the best of our ability, but he will walk with a limp and possibly need a cane." Everyone in the room gasps as the doctor continues. "Jeremy will need several months of rehabilitation because he will need to learn to walk again. It will be up to Jeremy how much physical labor he wants to put into his recovery. This is going to be very hard for Jeremy to accept. In addition, I expect some mental issues such as depression, anxiety, and perhaps withdrawal. I need you to be prepared. You're his support group."

"We need to be the ones to inform Jeremy about his injuries," the older doctor says. "If he asks about the surgery, try to avoid the question by saying something like you haven't spoken to the doctor yet. He'll be heavily sedated, so he shouldn't realize you are not answering his questions about the surgery. I know the news is devastating, so if you need to cry, do it before seeing Jeremy. But, remember, be positive for his sake. Now, we are going home to rest. We'll check on Jeremy in the morning and break the news to him. Good night."

There isn't a dry eye in the waiting room once the doctors leave. This accident will change Jeremy's life forever and transform the man they know into someone else. Ashley shivers because somehow she feels she will bear the brunt of it, and so will Devon.

Chapter 53

JEREMY

After the doctor leaves, Jeremy spends the rest of the day crying, refusing to see anyone. The following day, he moves to a private room. Jeremy still refuses to see anyone, and he spends blaming Ashley for his accident. She hadn't run off the day before when he told her he loved her. I know she still has feelings for me. If only she has said something, he thinks. I would have concentrated on my skiing and not on her.

On the third day, Jeremy knows what he has to do. He tells the doctor to tell everyone to go home except Ashley. He wants to see only her. Everyone is disappointed but agrees to stay until Ashley gives them an update.

Ashley walks into the room, stands at the foot of Jeremy's bed, and looks directly into his eyes.

"Aren't you going to say anything?" Jeremy asks.

"What's there to say? You've already made up your mind, and nothing I say will change it," Ashley replies.

"You sound pretty sure of yourself."

"Jeremy, I probably know you best of all your family and friends. So yes, I'm sure."

Jeremy takes a deep breath and lowers his eyes. "Ashley, you are a beautiful, vibrant woman. You don't need or deserve a disabled person. I want you to be happy. As much as I love you, I'm letting you go to live a full life with a healthy, complete man." Jeremy glances up at Ashley, who is glaring at him.

"Okay, Jeremy, but I want to ask for one thing. I want to be able to see Devon whenever I want."

"Okay, but why if we aren't together?"

"Because I love him almost as much as I love his father." Ashley turns and walks to the door. Opening it, she slowly turns around. "Jeremy, you said you would never intentionally hurt me."

"And I haven't," he replies.

"You just did for the second time." Ashley walks through the door, letting it close softly behind her.

She finally said she loves me. Jeremy ponders, tears flowing from his eyes. Too little, too late, as the saying goes. I am glad she still wants to see Devon. Ashley will bring calmness to his life from now on.

Now, I am going to prove the doctors wrong. I will work hard, skiing and surfing again, even if I can't climb mountains.

Chapter 54

ASHLEY

When Ashley leaves Jeremy's room, it takes all her strength not to burst into tears. Although she knew what Jeremy would say, Ashley hoped she was wrong. She walks into the waiting room, telling everyone Jeremy looks good but is fighting his demons.

"Wesley, what time is your flight?" Ashley asks.

Wesley can read her demeanor. "It's at 3:00. Would you like me to see if a seat is available?"

"Yes, please. Goodbye, everyone. I hope you have a safe trip home. Wesley, I'll be at the hotel. You can text me." Ashley leaves the waiting room and the hospital. In her room, she finally allows herself to cry. Wesley arranges a seat for her on his flight.

Six months go by at a snail's pace for Ashley. She refuses to return to Jackson, so Wesley assigns another architect to oversee the office building remodel. Ashley spends one evening a week with Devon and every weekend. The little boy asks about his papa. Devon was told about his father's accident, so Ashley tells Devon that Jeremy is still recovering. This alone tells Ashley that Jeremy hasn't contacted his son.

Ashley and G talk on the phone once a week. Jeremy's name is never mentioned until the beginning of the seventh month.

"Ashley," G says, "have you finished designing Jeremy's house?"

"Yes, G, I have. Are you ready to hire a contractor?"

"Ashley, Jeremy's gone, so I want you to come to build it now."

"I'm not sure I can," Ashley replies honestly.

"This is more than just the house. I spoke to Michelle. She has been diagnosed with breast cancer. She is scheduled for surgery in two weeks, and then there's chemotherapy and radiation. She and Mike believe it would be best for Devon to come here. I agree. They will have their hands full. Because of my age, Mike and Michelle want you to have temporary guardianship of Devon. I would like you to come to build the house, and we can share talking care of Devon."

"G, shouldn't Devon's father do that?" Ashley asks.

"Yes, but I do not know where he is, and he changed his phone number. So I don't know how to get in touch with him."

"Okay, G. Let me try to work something out with Wesley."

The following day, Ashley talks to Wesley. She agrees to move to Jackson, run the new office, and build Jeremy's house. However, Ashley insists it won't be permanent. She knows Jeremy will return someday, and she's not sure she wants to be in Jackson when that happens.

Ashley spends the next two weeks meeting with clients and transferring them to other architects. They process legal paperwork naming Ashley as a temporary guardian until Devon turns eighteen or Jeremy returns. Michelle packs most of Devon's toys and clothes. Ashley picks the items up and takes them to her apartment so they can be loaded onto the moving van along with Ashley's things. Finally, on Friday of the second week, Ashley picks up Devon, and they fly to Jackson to start their new temporary life.

Chapter 55

JEREMY

Jeremy spends six months in rehab. He builds his upper body strength in the first two months. The final four months are spent learning to walk. Jeremy is pleased with his progress, but he has a limp and must use a cane, just as the doctors predicted. That disappoints him greatly, but he is happy when he's cleared to fly.

The day after his release from rehab, Jeremy packs everything and moves out of G's house. He tells G goodbye but doesn't tell her where he's going. On the way to the airport, Jeremy purchases a new phone and gets a new phone number. He is leaving the ranch for good and returning to his old life of surfing, skiing anywhere but Jackson, partying, and women. He doesn't want to be contacted by anyone.

After they loaded everything onto the jet, Jeremy and Bill take off. Bill is sworn to secrecy about Jeremy's destination and will return on a commercial airline to Wyoming after their arrival wherever Jeremy plans to go. Once Jeremy takes off, he circles the ranch one last time. Tears come to his eyes, realizing his chances of seeing G and the ranch again are slim. And his chances of ever having a life with Ashley are gone.

Jeremy's friends and the women he's ever slept with are happy to see him back in Oaxaca. They were unaware of his accident and are shocked to see him limping and using a cane. Jeremy assures them he's fine and ready to get back on a surfboard.

The first week in Oaxaca is nothing but parties, booze and women for Jeremy. He doesn't sleep much because when he does, the black-haired beauty he loves always enters his dreams. Nothing he does can remove her from his mind when he's sober.

Finally, during his second week in Oaxaca, Jeremy tries to surf but cannot maintain his balance on the surfboard. He tries different boards and boogie boards but has no luck. At first, Jeremy's friends try to help him but give up when they see him struggling. Jeremy continues trying for several weeks, to no avail. Finally, his friends stop inviting him to hang out and go bar hopping. The women lose interest in the handsome former surfer and move on to other men.

Jeremy realizes that not only can he no longer surf, but he has become as "has been" in the surfing world. He becomes depressed and only leaves his condo to buy more liquor. His food, when he eats, is delivered to his door. He stares out the window mornings and evenings, watching his former friends and new people surf. Jeremy quickly discovers that liquor also keeps dreams of Ashley away.

Four months after his arrival in Oaxaca, Jeremy wakes up lying on his bathroom floor in vomit. He gets up and brews a large pot of coffee instead of reaching for a liquor bottle. Jeremy sits on the sofa drinking his coffee and decides Oaxaca is no longer his place. So after cleaning the bathroom, showering, and dressing, Jeremy calls a realtor. He places his condo on the market, fully furnished. Jeremy packs his clothes, loading them on his jet.

Since he wants to leave quickly, Jeremy doesn't hire a co-pilot. Instead, he flies himself to an airport near St. Moritz, Switzerland alone. Once there, he rents a car and drives to his favorite ski resort. The resort is busy, but Jeremy's recognized, and they find a room for him. Many of Jeremy's friends are there for ski season, and the women are plentiful.

Everyone is surprised by Jeremy's limp and use of a cane but welcomes him back into the group. But, again, partying, booze, and women occupy Jeremy's first week there. Jeremy watches his friends ski and snowboard. He remembers how easy skiing was and decides to try it himself, but he exercises caution. He drives to a smaller resort and attempts to ski but has no luck. His ankles won't support his weight on the skis, and his balance is off. Jeremy travels to the small resort every day for one month and tries. Finally, he gives up trying knowing his skiing days are over.

After another month, Jeremy's friends grow tired of his excuses not to ski with them and begin to evade him. Finally, the women become uninterested and leave Jeremy alone. Skiers and non-skiers avoid Jeremy Marsh, the former skiing sensation/playboy.

Contemplating his next move, Jeremy decides the only thing he has left that he can still do is his photography. Curious if anyone has contacted him with job offers, Jeremy goes to the resort's business center and logs into his email account. He deletes all emails from family and Wesley without reading them. Unfortunately, there are no emails from Ashley.

Jeremy finds three job offers, two of which have expired. However, the one sent a week ago interests Jeremy. The park service is interested in photos taken in the Smoky Mountains. Jeremy spends several hours researching the park located in Tennessee and North Carolina. Trails for hiking run throughout the park and camping is allowed. Although Jeremy has never been there, he recalls seeing the mountains when he accompanied Ashley to bury her mother. *Now, this I can do.*

First, Jeremy emails the park service. He will take the job and requests six months to do the work adequately. Next, he locates and hires a co-pilot to fly with him to Tennessee. Finally, Jeremy emails G, telling her he is doing well. That's all he says. By then, the park service replies, granting Jeremy's six-month request.

Chapter 56

ASHLEY

Ashley's first six months in Jackson are a whirlwind. Although four other architects are in the office, Ashley is busy with work. But, true to his word, Wesley hired an excellent office manager to run the place, taking the unwanted pressure off of Ashley. Ashley moved into the apartment above the offices, which is large enough for her and Devon. One month after arriving in Jackson, Ashley hired a contractor to build Jeremy's house. The work is going well and should be completed in nine months.

They diagnosed G with Arthritis which bothers her most in the morning. She and Ashley work it out, so Devon spends days with G and nights and weekends with Ashley. Since it is a forty-five-minute drive to the ranch, Hank, Ida, or G meet Ashley halfway in mornings and evenings to pick up or deliver Devon. The little boy loves the ranch, so he and Ashley spend Saturday nights at the line shack. Devon refers to it as camping out.

Once a month, Ashley takes Devon to Vegas to see Mike and Michelle for the weekend. This allows Ashley time to meet with Wesley and relax. Having a little boy is taxing, and the time in Vegas gives Ashley a much-needed break.

On a Tuesday morning, the first week of Ashley's seventh month in Jackson, the office receptionist lays a thick manila envelope on Ashley's desk. Ashley's name is the only thing on the envelope. When she questions the receptionist, the receptionist tells her it was delivered by courier.

Curious, Ashley opens the envelope and dumps the contents on her desk. The envelope contains copies of various legal documents and several photographs. Ashley carefully sorts through the papers, reading each one in its entirety. First, there is the birth certificate of her little brother. Second, there is the adoption paperwork where the Harrison's adopted her brother at age two. Third is the current residence of the Harrison's in Wyoming and a photograph of a middle-aged couple. The following items rock Ashley's world. First, there is a copy of the legal document changing her brother's name. Next is a DNA profile of Ashley and baby Harrison proving they are siblings. Finally, there is a current picture of Ashley's brother.

Ashley stares at the documents. Then she jumps up and copies everything, placing it into a new envelope. Next, she tells the receptionist that she is gone for the day. Ashley jumps into her car and drives to the ranch. When she gets there, Ashley asks Hank where the cowboys are. He replies in the valley with the cattle. Ashley jumps into the four-wheeler with the envelope and heads to the valley.

Tyler sees Ashley driving too fast toward the valley. He turns his horse and gallops to meet her, hoping she doesn't scare the cattle.

"Ashley, slow down," Tyler yells at her.

She stops the vehicle as he rides up beside her. "Tyler, I need to talk to you. It's very important."

"Okay, Ashley," he replies, getting down from his horse. "Let's sit on a boulder and talk."

"Tyler, tell me about your parents. I know it's a crazy request, but it's important."

"Well, my parents are Bill and Janet Harrison. They live on the other side of Jackson. They are my adoptive parents. I know nothing about my birth parents. I was adopted when I was two, and the Harrisons never talked about my real parents."

"Tyler, I need you to read over this paperwork," Ashley states as she hands him the envelope. His face is confused, but he opens the envelope and reads the paperwork.

Finally, he looks at Ashley and says, "wow. So according to this, you and I are brother and sister." Ashley nods. "But this DNA test really doesn't prove anything. I mean, how did someone get our DNA?"

"Actually, it's easier than you think. Whoever did this could have followed us and picked up a cup we drank out of and threw away."

"I still find it hard to believe."

"Tyler, you and I haven't had sex, have we?" Tyler shakes his head, a crease forming between his eyebrows. "I've never seen you naked, have I?"

"Not that I'm aware of. What are you getting at?"

Ashley smiles. "My little brother had a light tan birthmark covering almost his left butt cheek. I know. I changed his diaper more times than I care to remember."

"So do I," Tyler whispers, looking at Ashley through fresh eyes. "Ashley, I need time to digest this."

"Me, too," Ashley replies. "These are your copies. We can do a new DNA test if you like. Then, when you're ready, we can sit down and talk about our parents. It's a horrible story, but it can't be changed." Se squeezes Tyler's hand.

"You know it's funny. You're a beautiful woman, Ashley, but for some unexplainable reason, I never was interested in you. This might explain why. But, I have to ask, who did this?"

"I do not know, Tyler. The information just showed up at my office. Now, I'll let you get back to work. Can I hug you before I go?" Tyler nods, and the pair hug. Ashley gets into the four-wheeler as Tyler climbs back on his horse to join the other cowboys.

Chapter 57

JEREMY

After landing in Gatlinburg, Tennessee, Jeremy's co-pilot flies home. Jeremy rents a hanger for the jet and rents an SUV. He spends the next week buying camping equipment, food, permits and fees and planning his route through the park. Although there are trails throughout the park, Jeremy plans to stay off them as much as possible. Finally, he retrieves all the photography equipment he estimates he will need and decides to start his adventure the following Sunday.

The first few days are rough for Jeremy. He is out of shape, and his legs ache, so he doesn't make as much progress as he wanted. But each day gets a little easier for him. Some nights he sleeps in his tent, the rest in a sleeping bag on the ground. He tries to stop beside a stream each night to have fresh water. Then, knowing he has six months, Jeremy stops to photograph the beauty of the mountains, nature and wildlife, which there is a lot of. He enjoys the peacefulness of the park and has no technology.

Jeremy looks at his paper calendar and is surprised he only has one week left. He crawls into his sleeping bag, turns off his lantern, and looks at the clear sky. It reminds him of the times he and Ashley would lie on the ground and watch the stars. Ashley. She was always on his mind as much as he tried to forget her. *Ashley would like this*, or *I wish I could show this to Ashley*; Jeremy would think every time he spotted something new or different.

"I love that woman so much," Jeremy says aloud, talking to the stars. "But I blew it with her. She's in Vegas and probably married to some guy she met. She is the only woman I will ever truly love. Plus, she was my friend. My only friend, other than Wesley. All the people I thought were my friends just used me and hung around with me because I was an excellent skier or surfer."

Jeremy's inner voice, which has remained silent for over a year, speaks to him as he continues to look at the stars and breathe the fresh air. Jeremy, it's time to go home. You now know where home is. It's where you belong and where you need to raise your son. "Yes," Jeremy whispers. "I know my place, and I need to start being a real father to my little boy. So I will go there soon."

Chapter 58

ASHLEY

Ashley lies on the blanket and looks at the stars. It's Saturday night, and Devon is asleep in the line shack. *I've been here a year now,* she thinks. *The last six months have gone by fast. Jeremy's house is finished, so my commitment to G is complete. The architects are doing a fantastic job, and my role has become chiefly as an advisor. Tyler and I have a great relationship. He loves helping with Devon. Unfortunately, Michelle's cancer has returned and spread throughout her body. Her time is limited.*

There's no reason for me to stay here anymore. Wesley just opened a branch in Arizona. Perhaps it is time for me to go elsewhere and start a new life. At some point, Jeremy will return, and I will lose Devon. When I lose Devon, there will be no more ties to Jeremy and this ranch. Maybe I'll find a man I can love, but I'll love no one like Jeremy. He's that once-in-a-lifetime love you read about in books. He's also the man that's probably found a woman, fallen in love, and married her. They may have a child by now, for all I know. I can still bring Devon to see G once a month. Arizona isn't that far. I'll wait a week or so and then talk to Wesley.

Chapter 59

JEREMY

It's late when Jeremy's jet lands in Jackson, so he checks into a hotel for the night. He reviews the hundreds of pictures on the laptop he bought before leaving Tennessee. There was one other stop he made before boarding the jet. Jeremy took flowers to Ashley's mother's grave. He sat there a long time, wondering about Ashley. Wash she married? Was she still in touch with G? Was she still working for Wesley or had she opened her own firm? These were questions he would have to find out as soon as possible.

Since he stayed up late looking at photos, Jeremy sleeps until 9:00 am. Then he dresses and calls Hank to pick him up. He swears Hank to secrecy wishing to surprise G. When Jeremy walks in the door, G rushes to greet him, but Devon stays several feet away. After all, it's been a year since he's seen his papa. Jeremy sits in a chair and talks to the little boy for a long time. Finally, Devon warms up to him and rushes into his arms. Tears fill Jeremy's eyes, and he promises the little boy who just turned four he will never leave him like that again.

G tells Jeremy that Devon has a dentist appointment at 1:00 pm. She says she isn't feeling well and asks Jeremy to take Devon. Jeremy agrees happily, stating he and Devon will have lunch at Devon's favorite chicken tenders place.

As Jeremy and Devon walk out of the dentist's office, Devon says, "let's go see mama."

"Mama?" Jeremy says as his heart beats faster.

"Yes, that's her office," Devon replies, pointing across the street. The little boy doesn't wait for his papa to answer. Instead, he drags Jeremy across the street toward Ashley's office. Jeremy has to slow the little boy down because he can't keep up because of his limp.

Jeremy opens the door for Devon, who steps inside and yells, "mama" at the top of his lungs.

"I'm in the back, sweetheart," a voice so familiar to Jeremy answers. Devon takes off, running toward the back. He suddenly stops, returns to Jeremy, and grasps his hand, pulling him along. Jeremy drops Devon's hand before the little boy crosses the threshold into Ashley's office. Devon runs and jumps into Ashley's lap. "Hey, little man. I didn't know G was bringing you into town today," Ashley says, hugging Devon tightly.

"G didn't. Papa took me to the dentist."

Ashley slowly looks up into Jeremy's eyes. "Jeremy," she says.

"Hello, Ashley."

"Papa, come look at my office," Devon says, climbing off Ashley's lap. He runs to a door in her office and opens it. "Come on, papa."

"May I come in?" Jeremy asks. Ashley nods and waves her arm toward Devon.

Jeremy walks over and looks in the doorway. Devon has his very own little office, complete with a table, chair, and boxes of building blocks. An assortment of toy trucks set on shelves lining all the walls. "Wow, Devon, this is fantastic."

"Want to see my bedroom?" Devon asks.

"Maybe some other time. We need to get home. I can see I have much to talk to G about." Devon nods.

"Devon can stay here. That way, Hank won't have to bring him back later," Ashley says.

Jeremy looks at her in surprise, but Ashley looks down at her desk, writing on a legal pad. "Okay. See you tomorrow, Devon?" Jeremy says. Devon nods and sits down at his table full of building blocks. "It's nice to see you, Ashley." She shrugs and doesn't respond. Jeremy quietly leaves the room and office.

Jeremy and G spend the rest of the day talking. She tells him about her arthritis and Michelle's illness. She tells him that Michelle is in hospice care at home and that if Jeremy wants to see Michelle, he should do it quickly. G also tells him about

Ashley's temporary guardianship of Devon and how G and Ashley have worked things out, so Devon spends quality time with them. The one thing G doesn't tell Jeremy about is his house. It's not time yet, she determines.

Chapter 60

ASHLEY

Since Ashley was busy with Devon, she hadn't had time to think about Jeremy. But after she drops the little boy off with Hank, Ashley has time to think on the way to her office. Jeremy looks good, she thinks. His hair is longer, and he's a little thinner, but still just as handsome. Then, when I thought I was getting past the pain and loneliness, Jeremy shows up. It's been a little over a year. This speeds up my conversation with Wesley for sure.

At 11:00, the receptionist informs Ashley she has a visitor. She's not really surprised when Jeremy walks in. "I was expecting you to show up, but not this soon. So I guess you're here to talk about Devon," Ashley says as Jeremy sits in front of her desk.

"I didn't come to talk about Devon, but since you brought him up, we can talk about him. Ashley, I don't want to change anything, at least for a while. I've been gone a long time. Devon and I need to get to know each other again before I take over. Is that okay with you?" Jeremy asks.

"Thank you, Jeremy. Now, what can I do for you?"

"G told me about Michelle. I am planning to go to Vegas tomorrow to see her. I wanted to know if you would like to go with me?"

"Jeremy, that would be wonderful. Devon and I saw her two weeks ago. Mike said she is getting close to the end. I don't think we should take Devon, though. I would like him to remember Michelle the way she was."

"I agree. The news came as an immense shock to me. We can leave at 8:00 if that's okay. Devon can spend the night with me, so you won't have to meet Hank in the morning."

"Okay. Jeremy, I prefer we get two cars tomorrow. Michelle tires easily, and I need to spend some time with Wesley. So I suggest you see Michelle in the morning while I'm with Wesley and I'll see her in the afternoon," Ashley tells him.

"That sounds like a good idea. I'll see you at the airport in the morning. Goodbye, Ashley." Jeremy leaves the office without waiting for Ashley to say goodbye.

Great, I get to keep Devon for a while longer, she thinks as she does a little happy dance around the office. Jeremy's right. If it hadn't been for G showing Devon pictures of his father and telling stories, Devon would probably have forgotten Jeremy. So that was kind of Jeremy offering to take me to Vegas. I'll call Wesley to let him know I'll be there tomorrow morning.

Ashley pulls up to the hangar at 7:55, but doesn't see Jeremy. The door to the jet is open, so she makes her way up the stairs. At the top, Ashley is greeted by Bill, Jeremy's long-time co-pilot. She hasn't seen Bill since he picked her up in Seattle a year ago. They talk for a few minutes. Then Ashley heads to a seat at the back of the plane. Jeremy comes out of the bedroom, greets Ashley, and sits in the middle of the aircraft.

After the plane reaches cruising speed, Jeremy says, "Ashley, when you were a kid, did your parents take you to the Smoky Mountains?"

"Yes, we went a lot before my brother was born. We would camp sometimes and make day trips at other times. I loved it there so much." Ashley pauses. "I guess that's why I like the ranch so much. The clouds hanging low over the mountain tops, the fresh air and the stars remind me of the Smoky Mountains."

"I spend the last six months there taking photos. The park service gave me a contract to take pictures for their website. I liked it there because I was camping and living off the grid. I'm reviewing the photos to decide which ones to send them. I am considering buying a big screen TV for my bedroom to analyze them better."

Hmmm, Ashley thinks. It sounds like he doesn't know about the house yet. There is a wall in the office and in the living room where a TV would fit.

"Ashley, while I was in Tennessee, I visited your mother's grave and placed flowers there for you."

"Thank you, Jeremy. That was very kind of you to think of her."

"I was thinking of you," Jeremy whispers, but Ashley hears it. "Would you like to look at some pictures with me? Two eyes are better than one."

Looking at pictures on Jeremy's laptop would require sitting next to him. I can't do that, Ashley decides. "Maybe some other time, Jeremy," Ashley answers and returns to reading her book. My gosh, he thought of me. At least he didn't forget me while he was gone.

"At least I asked this time," Jeremy says, reminding Ashley of when he crashed into her apartment, expecting her to be available at his whim.

Chapter 61

JEREMY

Jeremy and Ashley split up when the jet arrives in Vegas. Ashley heads to see Wesley, and Jeremy visits Mike and Michelle's home. He is shocked by Michelle's appearance when he walks into the room. She is dozing, but wakes when Jeremy touches her hand as Mike looks on.

Apologizing for leaving as he did and not contacting Devon while he was away brings Jeremy to tears. He promises never to leave Devon like that again. Mike and Michelle talk about how excellent Ashley is with Devon, as if she was his birth mother. After an hour, Jeremy leaves with boxes of pictures of Devon and a few remaining clothes and toys.

Jeremy grabs a quick lunch and calls Wesley to ensure Ashley has left. Wesley says she has, so Jeremy drives to Wesley's office.

"Wesley, thanks for coming to the hospital. I apologize for not seeing you and not being in touch over the past year," Jeremy says, entering the office.

"Jeremy, I'm the last person you need to apologize to. I've known you a long time and knew what was going through your head. Now, is your head on straight?"

"It is. Jackson is my home and where I belong. While I was gone, I realized I only had two genuine friends and let one escape. Thanks for always being by my side."

"Speaking of your other friend, she was here this morning. Ashley requested a transfer to my new office in Arizona," Wesley says.

"What did you tell her?" Jeremy asks.

"I told her I would consider it, but no openings currently exist. She sounds determined to leave Jackson. You still love her, so you better do something quickly."

"If only I knew if she still loved me," Jeremy says sadly.

Wesley pauses and then says, "she does. Ashley doesn't have a life outside Devon. You have your work cut out for you, though."

The men talk longer, then Jeremy returns to the airport.

The flight back to Jackson is quiet. When they land, Jeremy asks Ashley if Devon can spend the night with him again since it is getting late. Ashley agrees. Then Jeremy asks Ashley if she would consider having dinner with him. Ashley tells him she has dinner plans with Tyler.

"I know seeing Michelle was hard, but I expected you to return in a good mood, having spent time with Ashley," G says as Jeremy makes a sandwich in the kitchen. "And I thought the two of you might have dinner together."

"Ashley's having dinner with Tyler," Jeremy says sadly.

"Ashley didn't tell you?"

"Tell me what?" Jeremy asks.

"She found out about six months ago that Tyler is her brother. One day an envelope showed up at her office with paperwork proving it," G says and then pauses. "Did you have something to do with that?"

"No, G. I didn't. But that's great news for Ashley and Tyler."

"It is. So you don't have to be jealous of Tyler anymore," G states, laughing as she leaves the room.

The following morning, G tells Jeremy she has something to show him. They leave Devon with Hank and Ida and drive to Jeremy's new house.

"Wow, this is beautiful," Jeremy says as they drive up to the house. "When are you moving in, G?"

"This is your house, Jeremy. I built it for you because I'm leaving the ranch to you. Ashley designed it and oversaw the construction."

"G, you don't have to leave the ranch to me."

"I want the ranch to stay in the family. You are the only one I trust to care for it. So now that you're back, I'll show you how to run it."

"Okay, G. Did Ashley really do this for me?" Jeremy asks in amazement as he and G walk into the house.

"Yes. I told her I was leaving the ranch to you and asked her to do it. She had finished the design before you left. Then built it after you were gone." The house is empty, but as he and G walk through it, Jeremy notices Ashley had incorporated all his dreams for a home, including a skylight in the master bedroom.

"I see little touches of Ashley throughout the house," Jeremy tells G.

"I'm not surprised. Ashley hoped to live here one day," G says. Jeremy turns away, so G won't see the tears filling his eyes. "Ashley made the house as self-sustainable as possible, given the location. Now, you need to buy furniture. Ashley and I wouldn't do it because this is yours and Devon's house to do as you please."

"G, could I be alone?" Jeremy asks, his voice shaky and his back to her. G says okay. Jeremy knows she's gone when he hears the four-wheeler drive away. Jeremy sits on the massive fireplace and sobs. Everything Ashley did was out of love for him. It is reflected in the house and the location. I must make things right and get her to trust me again.

Chapter 62

ASHLEY

Ashley is surprised when Jeremy calls to tell her he wants to meet with her, so he will bring Devon into town this afternoon. Her brain dreads seeing him again, but her heart beats with excitement. At 4:00, Jeremy and Devon walk into her office.

"Jeremy, thanks for bringing Devon home."

"Devon, why don't you work in your office while I talk to your mama?" Devon nods, goes into his office, and closes the door. "Ashley, G showed me the house this morning. It is everything I ever dreamed of and more. Thank you."

"You're welcome. What can I do for you?" Ashley asks, looking everywhere but at Jeremy.

"It looks like I need furniture."

"I have an excellent interior designer on staff. I know she'll be happy to help you."

"I want you to help as well. But first, I'll need help with Devon's room. Besides, I see touches of you through the house."

"It wasn't intentional; I assure you," Ashley states, knowing she is lying. The design was finished before Jeremy left, and Ashley refused to make changes. "I'll be happy to show you the self-sustaining items in the house. Would Saturday afternoon work for you? Devon and I spend Saturday nights in the line shack. Devon calls it camping out."

Jeremy ponders for a few moments and then says, "Saturday is good for me, but why don't you and Devon really camp out? I have a small tent Devon would love and other camping equipment. There are sleeping bags in the line shack. If it's okay with you, I'll find a place and set everything up for you."

"I think Devon would love that, but I haven't been camping since I was a kid. So I don't know how to do anything," Ashley says.

"I'll help if you don't mind. It will give me time to spend with Devon, but I promise not to interfere with your private time with him."

"Okay, Jeremy. That will be fine. We can tour the house first, so I'll see you around 3:00," Ashley says.

"Sounds good. Thanks, Ashley. Oh, by the way, I heard about Tyler. Congratulations! I know you are happy to have your brother finally."

"I am. He's been a big help with Devon while you were away." Ashley's voice breaks. "See you Saturday." Jeremy knows he's been dismissed, so he stands, tells Devon goodbye, and waves as he walks out the door.

Chapter 63

JEREMY

Before returning to the ranch, Jeremy swings by the airport and unloads all his camping gear into the SUV. He can feel excitement building in his body. Now he needs to make a plan.

Jeremy takes the four-wheeler the following morning, searching for the perfect camping spot. He finally finds it next to a stream and no trees overhead so Ashley, Devon, and hopefully, he can look at the stars together. Then Jeremy drives to the food store and buys food for dinner, breakfast and snacks that can be cooked on an open fire. That night, he loads everything on the four-wheeler. Jeremy plans to set everything up before meeting with Ashley at 3:00 the next day.

Ashley and Devon arrive promptly at 3:00. Ashley looks gorgeous in denim shorts that hit her mid-thigh, a green tank top, sneakers and her jet-black hair pulled into a ponytail. Looking at her, Jeremy closes his eyes and remembers how her body felt next to him when they made love.

"Papa, are we going camping?" the little boy asks excitedly.

"Yes, son. We are, but first, we need to tour the house. I think you need to pick out your bedroom." Devon giggles and runs through the house, looking at all four bedrooms. Ashley shrugs and follows him. "Devon, the big one is mine, but you can have your choice of the other three," Jeremy yells as he looks at Ashley. "Why four bedrooms?"

"Well, I assumed one day Devon might have siblings, and as they get older, they will want their privacy and their own room," Ashley replies.

"Hmmm, siblings for Devon. That's an interesting thought. Now show me the self-sustaining features of the house, please." It takes two hours for Ashley to show Jeremy all the features and how they work. He is very impressed and tells her so.

"Well, is everyone ready to go camping?" Jeremy asks. Devon squeals joyfully as Ashley goes to the line shack to collect several blankets. Then, the threesome climb into the four-wheeler and heads to the campsite.

As far as Jeremy knows, Ashley and Devon have never been to the part of the ranch he chose for the campsite. When they arrive, Devon heads for the tent, and Ashley looks around in wonder. Jeremy watches her for a few moments and then stands beside her. "Do you approve?" he asks.

"Oh, Jeremy. This is absolutely spectacular." Ashley watches as two bald eagles circle overhead. "It is so quiet. I can hear the stream running. I think Devon will put you in charge of selecting camping spots from now on." Ashley looks up for so long that when she looks down, she's dizzy and almost stumbles. Jeremy catches her with his hands on her waist before she can fall. Ashley says thanks and then walks toward the tent to check on Devon.

Jeremy brought a Frisbee, and the three plays until Jeremy starts the fire for dinner. Jeremy chose hotdogs because he believed Devon would enjoy roasting them over the open fire. Smores are desserts.

It's dark by the time dinner is finished. Jeremy lays a blanket on the ground so they can look at the stars. Devon lies between Jeremy and Ashley, looking at the sky while Jeremy points out different constellations. Devon asks many questions as he listens intently, but soon grows quiet.

"Devon's fallen asleep," Jeremy whispers. "I'll put him to bed. You stay here and relax." When Jeremy returns, he places two more logs on the fire. "Ashley, may I lie down on the blanket with you?" She nods, so Jeremy lies close but doesn't touch her. "Did you come out to the ranch and look at the stars while I was gone?"

"Every Saturday night after Devon went to sleep," Ashley replies.

"I bet we looked at the same stars." Jeremy pauses. "I wonder if we thought the same things."

"I doubt it, Jeremy," Ashley replies. "I wondered why you left, why you hurt me twice, why I came back, and what I would do when you got back if I was still here."

"That's a lot to wonder."

"I had plenty of time," Ashley huffs.

"Did you come up with any answers?" Jeremy asks, rolling on his side to look at her, fighting the urge to touch her creamy skin.

"Only why I came back. I promised to build your house. I planned to leave as soon as it was finished. Then Michelle got sick. Devon needed to be cared for, and I needed him."

"You've been a wonderful mother to him, Ashley. He loves you so much. I have been a miserable father, but I plan to spend the rest of my life making it up to him." Jeremy pauses, trying to find the words to say. "Do you feel like listening while I try to explain myself?"

"I suppose so. This conversation would probably happen sooner or later, so go ahead," Ashley answers.

"The first time I hurt you was because I was scared. I had feelings and emotions that were so unfamiliar to me. I didn't know what I wanted, and I guess I wasn't ready to grow up. Then, I realized I had fallen in love with you and wanted you so much. That's why I came back. I wanted to tell you how I felt, and I did, but you left without a word."

"I did, didn't I? Did you think you could walk back into my life and things would be the same?" Ashley asks.

"I had hoped so. When I went down the ski slope, I was thinking of you and how to get you back. I wasn't paying attention to my skiing. Then the accident happened. I had to let you go as I told you because you didn't and still don't deserve a disabled person like me."

"I guess I should thank you for deciding my life for me," Ashley says sarcastically.

"Okay, I deserve that. Anyway, I left because I wanted to prove the doctors wrong and prove that I could still do the things I enjoyed. But I quickly realized I couldn't and would never be able to. I also discovered my friends weren't really friends at all. They just hung around with me because of the name I made for myself, surfing and skiing. My so-called friends deserted me when I could no longer do those things."

"I'm sorry, Jeremy."

"Don't be. I realized that you and Wesley were the only people that accepted me for me. My name and my money meant nothing to you. But I had lost you as a result of my stupidity. I realized I could still do the one thing I enjoyed most, photography. I got a job offer for the Smoky Mountains, and I took it. For six months, I avoided people and technology. It was just me and nature. Then, one night, I looked at my calendar. I had one week left."

"Jeremy, you don't have to tell me all this," Ashley says.

"But I do, Ashley. I want you to understand. That night I lay in my sleeping bag looking at the stars like we're doing now. Suddenly, I knew where I was supposed to be. I know where home was. I knew it was time to be a real father to Devon. But the most important thing of all was that I love you and always will."

"Oh, Jeremy. Again, do you think you can just walk into my life and everything be the same as it was? I'm a different person now. I'm not the naïve twenty-six-year-old virgin I was when you met me. I'm not the same woman that believed in the fairy tale endings of happily ever after," Ashley says.

"I know you're not. You're stronger, and you've grown much like I have. But I believe that underneath all that you've become, you still love me as much as I love you."

"What if I do, Jeremy? I'm not strong enough to be hurt by you a third time. I won't let myself. I've already talked to Wesley about a transfer away from here and away from you."

"Ashley, please don't go. Please give me a chance. I'm not going anywhere. G said she is leaving the ranch to me, and I will start learning how to run it. And Ashley, you're Devon's mother now. Can you just up and leave him and move away? You know how hard it was for him to be shuffled between Mike, Michelle, and me." Jeremy reaches over and brushes her lip with his fingertips like he used to.

"Good night, Jeremy," is all Ashley says. She stands, grabs her sleeping bag, drags several feet away, and crawls inside. She turns her back to Jeremy.

Jeremy grabs his sleeping bag and places it in front of the tent to be there if Devon needs him.

Chapter 64

ASHLEY

If only Jeremy had stayed gone. If only he hadn't touched me. If only I still didn't love him. All these questions come to Ashley's mind as she lies in her sleeping bag. My heart says to give him another chance, but my brain says don't trust him. He's right about Devon, though. Can I really leave that precious little boy I love like my own? These questions and more keep Ashley awake most of the night. She wakes early to the smell of bacon and finds Devon in the sleeping bag beside her. Ashley doesn't open her eyes, but wraps her arms around the little boy. No, I can't leave him. No matter what happens between Jeremy and me, she decides.

"Mama, wake up. Papa's making breakfast on the fire," Devon says, wiggling in Ashley's arms. "He used water from the stream to make coffee."

"Well, I better go and try a cup. What did papa bring you to drink?"

"I have orange juice," Devon says proudly.

"Let's get up and go to the stream. We need to wash our faces," Ashley tells the little boy.

"I already did. Papa took me, and I peed too, just like a big boy." Ashley laughs, pushes Devon out of the bag, and then gets up.

"Good morning, Ashley," Jeremy says warily.

"Jeremy. I'll be right back." He tosses her a roll of toilet paper and looks away.

After a hearty breakfast of bacon, scrambled eggs, and homemade biscuits courtesy of Jeremy, Devon, and Jeremy go to the stream to fish. Jeremy bought a child's fishing rod just for the occasion. Ashley sits on the bank and watches as Jeremy teaches the boy how to use the rod. Then Jeremy joins Ashley.

"You look deep in thought," he says.

"Jeremy, I don't know what will happen, but I know I can't leave Devon," Ashley replies, looking him in the eyes for the first time since he returned.

"I know. He grows on you, doesn't he? Besides, he needs two parents. So we'll work out arrangements." Ashley nods.

Chapter 65

ASHLEY & JEREMY

The next three months go by quickly for Ashley and Jeremy. Ashley and Jeremy decorate the house with the interior designer from Ashley's office. A large screen TV is installed in the office and the living room first, so Jeremy can review his pictures. Ashley agrees to help, and Jeremy submits fifty photos to the park service. At Ashley's suggestion, Jeremy publishes various books showcasing his travels and photographs.

Ashley and Jeremy agree to a date night once a week while G watches Devon. At first, there is a tension between them, but it quickly dissipates, and they begin enjoying each other's company. Finally, they kiss, but it never moves past Jeremy's second kind of kiss because he doesn't want to rush Ashley.

At the beginning of the fourth month, Jeremy shocks Ashley by suggesting she move into one of the spare bedrooms. He says it will be easier for both of them to raise Devon. Ashley is at a point where she can work most of the week remotely, so she agrees. Devon is ecstatic to have both parents in the same house. It works well for Jeremy and Ashley because they share cooking and chores. It also allows Jeremy more time to spend with Devon. They do things such as playing catch, fishing, horseback riding and many other things Jeremy discovers he can do with his limp.

One late evening, Jeremy and Ashley sit around the fire pit, watching Devon ride in his battery-operated truck. Finally, Devon drives his truck to the fire pit and says, "I want a little sister." Ashley spits coffee all over her herself as Jeremy watches.

"Well, Devon, talk to your mama about that," Jeremy replies, trying not to laugh. "I'm ready any time, but your mama makes those kinds of decisions."

"Mama, can I have a little sister?"

"Devon, where did you get that idea?" Ashley asks. Jeremy observes the discussion with a smile.

"Mable, the cow had a boy and a girl. You and papa have a boy. So it's time for a girl," Devon states unabashedly. "You and papa have to sleep in the same room, though."

"Oh, my gosh! Jeremy, what have you been showing Devon and telling him?"

"We live on a ranch, Ashley. Cows have babies. I didn't have the talk with him, if that's what you're asking," Jeremy replies.

Ashley looks between Jeremy and Devon for a few seconds and then says, "Devon, your papa, and I need to discuss this privately. Your wanting a sister is very serious business."

"Okay," Devon replies and drives off.

Jeremy reaches for Ashley's hand and clasps it. "I have to agree with Devon. I think it's time."

"You're more interested in the process than an actual baby," Ashley says.

"What's wrong with that? Besides, I know you want to sleep with me. I can see it in your eyes and feel it in your body when we kiss."

"I suppose we could try."

"Try what? Sleeping in the same room or making a baby?" Jeremy grins, wiggling his eyebrows.

Ashley smiles slightly. "Hmmm, we've slept in the same bed before without making a baby."

"True, but I want all of you, Ashley." Jeremy gets down on one knee in front of her. "I want you forever and to make lots of babies with you. Will you share the rest of your life with me?"

"Are you proposing?" Jeremy nods. Ashley looks at him with love in her eyes. "I will under one condition." A crease forms between Jeremy's eyebrows. "That we start on the baby-making tonight."

About Author

Gaylene Nunn is a widowed 60+ year old woman who spent her career in banking, financial services, municipal government, and most recently as CFO for a upper level regional university that she helped create. She retired in 2017 with the title of Vice President Emeritus. Gaylene is a Texas native who enjoys reading, writing, traveling, and spending time with her dog, Sam, and cat, Emily.

Also By

A Second Chance at Love

Reclaimed Assurance

Forty Years too Late?

Before Your Loved One Goes—Planning for Your Reality

*Damaged by Love

*An Eternity of Love

*Co-authored with Deserie LaCrosse